W9-CUL-662

Hey, TodaysGirls! Check out 2day's kewlest music, books, and stuff when u hit *spiritgirl.com*

Published in Nashville, Tennessee, by Tommy Nelson®, a division of Thomas Nelson, Inc.

Scripture quotations are from the *International Children's Bible®, New Century Version®:* Copyright © 1986, 1988, 1999 by Tommy Nelson®, a division of Thomas Nelson, Inc.

Creative director: Robin Crouch
Storyline development & series continuity: Dandi Daley Mackall
Computer programming consultant: Lucinda C. Thurman

Library of Congress Cataloging-in-Publication Data

Peacock, Nancy.
    Power drive / written by Nancy Been Peacock ; created by Terry Brown.
      p. cm. – (TodaysGirls.com ; 10)
    Summary: Maya finds out about dirty politics when she decides to run for the student council.
    ISBN 0-8499-7713-4
    [1. Elections—Fiction. 2. Politics, Practical—Fiction. 3. High schools—Fiction. 4. Schools—Fiction.] I. Brown, Terry, 1961- II. Title. III. Series.

PZ7.P31175 Po 2001
[Fic]—dc21
                                        00-054893

Printed in the United States of America
01 02 03 04 05 PHX 9 8 7 6 5 4 3 2 1

POWER DRIVE

WRITTEN BY
Nancy Been Peacock

CREATED BY
Terry K. Brown

Thomas Nelson, Inc. • Nashville

Web Words

2 to/too

4 for

ACK! disgusted

AIMP always in my prayers

A/S/L age/sex/location

B4 before

BBL be back later

BBS be back soon

BD big deal

BF boyfriend

BFN bye for now

BRB be right back

BTW by the way

CU see you

Cuz because

CYAL8R see you later

Dunno don't know

Enuf enough

FWIW for what it's worth

FYI for your information

G2G or **GTG** I've got to go

GF girlfriend

GR8 great

H&K hug and kiss

IC I see

IN2 into

IRL in real life

JK just kidding

JLY Jesus loves you

JMO just my opinion

K okay

Kewl cool

KOTC kiss on the cheek

L8R later

LOL laugh out loud

LTNC long time no see

LY love you

NBD no big deal

NU new/knew

NW no way

OIC oh, I see

QT cutie

RO rock on

ROFL rolling on floor laughing

RU are you

SOL sooner or later

Splain explain

SWAK sealed with a kiss

SYS see you soon

Thanx (or) **thx** thanks

TNT till next time

TTFN ta ta for now

TTYL talk to you later

U you

U NO you know

UD you'd (you would)

UR your/you're/you are

WB welcome back

WBS write back soon

WTG way to go

Y why

(Note: Remember that capitalization may vary.)

chapter.1

The door to Maya's room flew open as if a bomb had been detonated in the hall.

"Hey!" Morgan exploded. "Do you know what time it is?"

Maya turned in her swivel desk chair and glanced at the clock on her bedside table. The red LCD numbers said 7:15 A.M. Only fifteen minutes to get to swim practice on time. But Maya wasn't about to let her younger sister see her panic.

"I'll be downstairs in a minute," she said, trying to sound bored.

Morgan bugged her eyes at Maya. "Yesterday I had to sneak into swim practice because I was so late. I can't be late two days in a row!"

Maya swiveled her chair back to the computer screen. Lately, she had become hypnotized by a new Web site. But this site was not about her usual favorites—makeup or fashion tips. It was about Karen Dean-Malloy, the United States senator from Indiana.

Everything about Karen Dean-Malloy exuded confidence—her posture, friendly eye contact, and firm handshakes. Even the senator's navy blue pinstripe suit carried an air of authority.

"OK, that is one classy look," Maya said to herself. "The woman has serious style."

A flashing box on the site caught Maya's eye:

Chat live with Sen. Dean-Malloy at votedean__malloy.org.

Maya clicked the box and read the chat in progress: questions and answers about budgets and healthcare costs for senior citizens.

"Bor-ring!" Maya chimed aloud. At the first opportunity, she typed in her question:

What kind of car do you drive?

Maya hit *Send* and sat back to wait for a response. *It's a good thing I got ready for school before I logged on,* she told herself.

Morgan stomped into the room. "If we don't leave right now—" she began.

"Fine, Miss Early Bird," Maya cut her short with an irritated wave of the wrist. "I'm signing off."

On the screen was Karen Dean-Malloy's response to her question:

I drive a VW Beetle. Fuel-efficient cars are a necessity for clean air in Indiana.

Maya smiled and hit *Quit*. *This is my kind of politician*, she told herself.

A late October chill hung in the morning air. Maya cranked the engine of her '72 Volkswagen Beetle, Mr. Beep, and listened to it whine a few times before firing into action.

"Yes, my little Beepster!" Maya cooed as she threw the gearshift into reverse and backed down the driveway. The tailpipe on the ice blue car clattered like a cowbell.

"This car gets noisier by the day," Morgan moaned.

Maya stiffened at her sister's criticism. "I'll have you know that Karen Dean-Malloy drives a Volkswagen Beetle."

Morgan seemed unimpressed. "Karen whoody-who?"

It was just like Morgan to not pay any attention to politics, Maya decided. Morgan loved animals and children, but so far, her interest in adult topics was nearly nonexistent.

"Dean-Malloy," Maya repeated as though she were speaking to a roomful of kindergartners. "United States senator from Indiana. On the cutting edge of national politics. And environmental issues—if that's the only thing that impresses you."

"Oh," Morgan replied flatly, letting her head fall against the car window in utter boredom.

Maya glanced quickly at her sister before returning her eyes to the road. "OK, fine, Morgan. You go ahead and save the whales or rescue a cat out of a tree or whatever it is you think is important. But I think politics is the future. The decisions made in Washington, D.C., affect the whole world, including Edgewood, Indiana."

Morgan rolled her eyes and sighed. "Here we go again. Last month, you were going to be the next Donna Karan. Fashion designer diva of the twenty-first century . . ."

Ouch. Morgan was right about that, Maya admitted. It had only been a few weeks since she had made that very declaration at the dinner table. And as usual, her parents had been completely supportive.

"My daughter, the famous designer," Dad had said beaming. "Go for it, Maya."

Predictably, Mom had taken the more practical approach. "We could get you started with some design courses at the college. Then we can check out some schools in the city."

"The college" was Edgewood Community College, where Maya's mom taught art history. "The city" was New York City, where Maya and her siblings had been born. When their mother's parents died, they left the house in Edgewood to their only child. Maya's parents had chosen to move the family to the small-town atmosphere of Edgewood, Indiana. The decision still rankled Maya every now and then. Why should she be stuck in this sleepy backwater village when she could be living a trend-setter's existence in New York City?

Lost in thought, Maya almost missed the turn into the student parking lot at Edgewood High School. Once Mr. Beep was neatly parked in his favorite spot overlooking the athletic field, the girls grabbed their swim team bags and headed for the pool.

They had just entered the chlorine-scented inner hallway when Amber emerged from the locker room, fully dressed. Maya was confused. Her best friend was always on time for any event. Why wasn't she ready for practice?

"Don't bother to get wet," Amber said, grinning slyly at Maya's confusion. "We have to be in the guidance counselors' office in about five minutes."

Oh, no! Coach was not going to like this. Maya had skipped yesterday's practice to finish her French homework because she had forgotten her textbook at school over the weekend. She and Amber had signed up for these college-counseling appointments more than a month ago. Back then, missing one swim practice had not seemed so important. But now she realized she'd have to miss two in a row.

Maya looked at Morgan, and before she could open her mouth, Morgan grinned. "I'll cover for you."

"You're the best," Maya said over her shoulder as Morgan walked past. "I owe you."

Morgan nodded silently and disappeared into the locker room.

"So why are you guys late this morning?"

Amber's question brought Maya back to her new favorite subject. As the two girls made their way to the guidance offices, Maya described the Karen Dean-Malloy Web site.

"The political process is where all the power is," Maya said, adopting an official Karen Dean-Malloy tone in her voice. "Decisions made in Washington involve the whole world. The more I think about it, the more I would like to be part of that decision-making process."

Amber bit her lip, clearly trying not to laugh. "Does this mean you no longer want to be the next host of the *Today Show*? Or no, wait! That was before you wanted to take over the fashion industry."

Ouch again. "OK, guilty as charged," Maya said, slightly wounded. "I guess I'm not allowed to dream big. I'll just resign myself to sweeping floors at the Gnosh Pit for the rest of my life."

Maya's dad owned the Gnosh Pit, a popular '50s-style diner, where Maya, her sister, and their friend Jamie often worked.

"Oh, stop it," Amber said, playfully nudging Maya's shoulder. "Hey, maybe it's a good thing you found your career choice before this morning. Mrs. Haferd can give you some guidance about which college to choose for a career in politics."

Maya brightened. "Yeah, you're right. So what do you think you want to do with your life?"

Amber shrugged. "My parents really want me to go to college, so I guess that's where I'm going. After that, who knows?"

The doors to the guidance offices were open. Maya smiled her goodbye at Amber and knocked on Mrs. Haferd's open door.

"Come in, Maya," the grandmotherly guidance counselor called, looking up from her paperwork. "I was just going over your academic file."

Mrs. Haferd had reached retirement age but had stayed on the Edgewood faculty an extra year. She knew many of the students by name and reminded Maya of a hen, clucking encouragingly at her chicks.

"On the form you filled out when you made this appointment, you said you wanted to get into broadcasting," Mrs Haferd began. "I've found several universities with good mass com departments," Mrs. Haferd began. "A communications degree would give you excellent preparation for a career in broadcasting."

Maya smiled and shook her head. "No thanks. I'm more interested in running for the United States Senate."

The "mother hen" looked at Maya as though she had just discovered one of her chicks had turned neon purple. "The Senate?" she echoed.

Maya smiled warmly and nodded. "So. What degree would I need for that?"

Mrs. Haferd still seemed bewildered. "Well, uh, political science, I suppose. Or maybe a pre-law degree, with the idea of going to a good law school after graduation . . ."

Maya briefly considered the possibility of those degrees. "No offense, Mrs. Haferd, but those sound awfully boring. Isn't there anything interesting I could study in college to prepare for a career in politics?"

"Well, yes," Mrs. Haferd said, choosing her words carefully. "But no matter what major you choose, there is one thing you need to know. People who serve in public office are very active in community organizations. And they tend to be leaders in those groups. Certainly the better colleges would want to see that type of activity on your application. It might even make you eligible for a college scholarship."

"OK," Maya said, warming to the subject. "Do you mean that I should run for city council or something like that?"

Mrs. Haferd smiled and patted Maya's hand. "Well, I think you might want to start with something more, uh, immediate. Student council elections are right around the corner. Why not try that?"

Maya tried to hide her disappointment. Student council did tedious things like sponsor dances or sell popcorn to raise money to send representatives to the annual state student council in Indianapolis. Where was the excitement in that?

"Let me give that some thought," Maya said, mentally crossing the idea off her list of possibilities.

The best thing about government class was that Maya's closest friends had all ended up in the same section. In addition to Amber, Jamie and Bren had both registered for Mr. Wallace's government class. Jamie and Bren, although best friends, couldn't be more opposite; Jamie was as shy and casual in her fashion taste as Bren was outgoing and decked out in the latest styles.

"What about *my* uniform?" Jamie was saying, pointing to the straight-legged Levi's she wore to school most days.

"Oh, come on, Jamie." Bren laughed. "It wouldn't kill you to dress up once in a while."

Maya dropped her books on a nearby desk. "What's this about?"

Bren grinned. "Some kids heard a rumor about a new dress code. And Jamie is terrified that she'll have to live without her jeans."

Maya considered this new turn of events. "What kind of a dress code? Like uniforms or what?"

"I don't know, but I don't like it," Jamie said with a pout. "I don't want to have to think about what to wear every single day of school or worse, have to wear a uniform."

Mr. Wallace entered the room and set his briefcase on his desk. As he snapped open its latches, he said, "Well, it sounds like you've gotten a head start on today's first topic."

Mr. Wallace hailed from Montana, and every time he spoke, Maya felt like she was watching a John Wayne movie. She kept waiting for him to call the students "pardners."

"At the faculty meeting yesterday," he continued, his accent thicker than molasses in a blizzard, "Mrs. Clark mentioned a possible dress code. I wondered what the students would think about it."

Maya looked at Jamie, but Jamie shook her head silently. Getting Jamie to share her opinions in class was like trying to coax a clam out of its shell.

"I would certainly like to make my views known," said a voice behind Maya. Camille Bates was never afraid to share her opinions. In fact, the hardest part with Camille was getting her to occasionally stop sharing her opinion. Maya had spent her freshman year—what had seemed like an eternity—on the debate team with Camille.

And then, as luck would have it, they were both cast into chorus roles as sophomores, and Maya had to endure Camille's incessant bragging throughout the entire production of *The Music Man*.

"Well, Camille," Mr. Wallace said. "Do you think Edgewood should have a dress code?"

Camille leaned back in her chair as if she were fielding questions from a panel of Supreme Court judges.

"It seems to me," Camille began, and her nostrils flared as she scented her argument, "that this dress code is a violation of our human rights. Why should we be forced to wear one style of clothing? Why can't we express ourselves through our own fashion choices? I've worked hard to build a designer-label wardrobe that expresses who I am. Is the administration planing to force us all to look like clones?"

If she keeps talking, Maya told herself, *I'm gonna turn around and throw up all over her designer shoes.* Maya looked across the aisle and locked eyes with Bren, who was resting her chin in her hand. She subtly pressed her pinky fingers against the inner rims of her own nostrils and stretched them in imitation of Camille's pulsating ones.

Maya ducked her head to hide her laughter, but her shaking shoulders gave her away.

"And that is why I am running for student council," Camille rambled on, her nostrils twitching like butterfly wings. "I believe I can represent the students well—and keep their human rights from being violated."

Even Mr. Wallace looked weary from Camille's campaign speech—like he'd been out on the trail for days roping stray cattle. "Well thank you, Camille. Does anyone else have an opinion?"

As if it had a mind of its own, Maya's hand flew into the air. "I don't think human rights have anything to do with a dress code. But I would like to know what this dress code is all about. Are we talking uniforms? What exactly did Mrs. Clark say?"

Mr. Wallace looked thoughtful. "She didn't get into the details. Maybe we should come back to this subject when we have more information," he said. "Let's switch gears and start a new section on the balance of power in federal government. Please turn to page one-fifty in your books."

A little later, Maya was seated in the cafeteria, peeling away the plastic wrap off a chef salad, when Amber sat down with her tray.

"Hey, you sounded like a born politician in government class today," Amber said. "Why don't you run for student council?"

Maya wrinkled her nose. "I can't stand all of those Camille

Bates types. They're constantly making speeches and posing for their campaign posters."

"What do you think it's like in the real world?" Amber asked. "Better get used to it before you decide to run for the Senate."

"Speaking of the perpetual candidate, here she comes," Maya mumbled.

Camille was making her way through the lunchroom, her entourage of girlfriends in tow. To Maya's surprise, they chose the next table and sat down. Maya busied herself with spearing a chunk of carrot and some torn lettuce.

"Let's move," Amber said quietly. "I don't think I can take a whole lunch hour of speech making."

"And miss Camille's latest pearls of wisdom?" Maya replied quietly. "I wouldn't dream of moving."

The speech making had already begun. "Of course, in a democracy there are always at least two sides to every issue," Camille droned on—her nostrils demonstrated by quivering independent of each other. "Even those who believe in restricting what students can wear to school should be allowed to have their say. Although it does seem un-American to me to restrict our clothing choices. I think those people who want to learn more about the dress code really just want to kiss up to the principal."

Maya gritted her teeth. She knew when she was being baited. *Don't fall for it,* she warned herself.

"I think that certain students need the approval of the

administration," Camille said, and her right nostril pounded out five syllables for ad-min-is-tra-tion. "But I would rather represent the students. Let other people score brownie points with the administration." Her left nostril pounded that time.

Maya put down her fork and stared at Camille. "Didn't you just say there are at least two sides to every issue?"

"Oh hi, Maya," Camille said sweetly. "Were you listening to our conversation?"

"Your conversation?" Maya echoed. "I didn't hear anyone talking but you. On and on and on and on."

Camille smiled again. "You know, Maya, it's very easy for you to sit on the sidelines and make fun of the people who want to take an active role in student government. But it takes real courage to run for office. Why aren't you running for office? Are you afraid to try?"

"Afraid? Who said I was afraid?" Maya stood up and walked toward Camille's table.

Camille stood up calmly and faced Maya. "So what's stopping you?"

"Not the possibility of losing to you," Maya replied. "I think most people can tell the difference between a phony and a real representative."

Camille smiled. "And which one are you?"

Maya stuck her finger in Camille's face. "You just made a huge mistake, Camille. So you want an opponent in this election? Well, you just got one. Maya Cross is officially running for student council!"

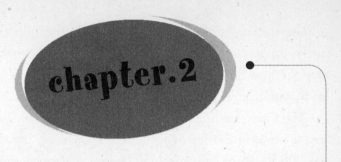

chapter.2

Maya rapped on the principals' door and walked cautiously into the antiseptic office. Mr. Carson and Mrs. Clark, the co-principals of Edgewood High School, looked up from the stacks of papers on Mr. Carson's desk.

"I'm sorry to barge in like this," Maya said, struggling to catch her breath. "But I need to know how to become a candidate for student council." She and Amber had charged out of the cafeteria, leaving their food on the table, and stormed to the office in a flurry of righteous indignation.

Mr. Carson smiled. "Petitions are out on the counter. You'll need to get fifteen signatures. And you'd better get cracking. The deadline is three o'clock this afternoon."

"Thanks," Maya said, exuding confidence. "You'll have it by three o'clock then."

Maya turned to leave, but Mrs. Clark held up her hand like a traffic cop signaling a car to stop. "I'm curious, Maya," she said in her clipped, all-business style. "Why did you wait until now to become a candidate?"

The question caught Maya off guard. There was no way she could tell Mrs. Clark that her candidacy amounted to a grudge match with Camille Bates. She had to think of a better reason. And fast. Something civic-minded perhaps?

"Well," Maya said, formulating her answer as she spoke, "I heard about the dress code, and it made me want to run for student council. You know, to be involved, help make decisions?"

Mr. Carson and Mrs. Clark looked at each other and nodded approvingly.

"Fair enough, Maya," Mrs. Clark said, making it sound as though Maya had passed some unwritten test. "I suppose you know the dress code was my idea. I've been reading a lot about this issue. Did you know that students behave better and get higher grades when there's a dress code?"

Maya was genuinely impressed. "No, I didn't know that."

Maya studied Mrs. Clark's outfit; it was a business suit with conservative pumps. On the other hand, Mr. Carson was a case study in the casual mode: a blue broadcloth shirt, no tie, and khaki slacks.

Mr. Carson grinned. "I do my best work when I'm comfortable," he said. "And I believe the students need to make responsible choices about their own style of dress."

When Mrs. Clark didn't respond, Maya nodded and smiled. "Well, you've both given me a lot to think about. Thanks again."

As the girls left, they stopped and took a petition from the counter. Once outside in the hallway, Maya breathed a sigh of relief. "I guess we should have known. This whole dress code idea came from Mrs. Clark."

"Hey, I'm impressed," Amber said. "You managed to agree with both of them. And you don't even have an opinion yet."

Maya stopped walking. "You know, you're right," she said. "How did I do that?"

Amber shrugged. "Maybe hanging out at the Karen Dean-Malloy Web site has been a good thing. Do you need a campaign manager?"

"No, I've already got someone," Maya deadpanned as Amber signed her petition. "Her name is Amber Thomas. She's got a real future in political strategy. One of the top advisers in Edgewood, I hear."

"Wow," Amber said, barely hiding her smile. "I would hire her in a flash. Is she very expensive?"

Maya nodded. "Her contract calls for unlimited chicken sandwiches at the Gnosh. Could run into the millions."

"Dollars or sandwiches?" Amber asked innocently.

"Chickens!" answered Maya. The girls broke into laughter that was drowned out by the loud, irritating buzzer signaling the end of lunch.

"We'll see how many names I get in my afternoon classes," said Maya.

Amber clenched her fist in a gesture of support. "You get 'em, girlfriend!"

In French class, Maya picked up eight more signatures. It was even easier than she had imagined. All she had to do was casually mention that she was running against Camille Bates for class representative.

"I got your back," said Raj Chowdhury. Raj, a lacrosse player, sat beside Maya in French class. "I'll vote for anyone who can silence Camille Bates. Her mouth's bigger than the Arc de Triomphe."

"*Merci beaucoup,*" said Maya, stuffing the petition in her book bag. "I'll give it my best shot."

In chemistry, Maya studiously avoided Bethany Troyer and Brittany Mertz. They were lab partners and staunch members of Camille's entourage.

Maya hid the petition inside her lab workbook and made her way around the room, gathering signatures. All the students, wearing lab aprons and goggles, were bent over their chemistry experiments. It was like scuba-diving through a coral reef, looking for friendly faces behind the goggles.

"Ryan?" Maya asked, treading over to Amber's brother, and his lab partner, Darryl Hume. "Would you sign my petition? I'm running for student council, and I need fifteen signatures by the end of today."

Ryan elbowed Darryl. "Whaddaya think, Darryl? Should we sign Maya's petition? I hear she's willing to let us copy all of her lab reports in exchange for our signatures."

Darryl made a face at Ryan and shook his head in disgust. "Way to go, Ryan. You'll get Maya disqualified before she even turns in her petition."

Darryl smiled as he turned back toward Maya, "You can have my support any time you want it."

Maya felt herself blush, and she fought back a smile. Being a candidate was a great excuse to flirt. "Thanks, Darryl. Every vote's important in this election. I'm running against Camille Bates."

Darryl flexed his nostrils. "You mean Bat-Cave-Bates?"

Wow! This was going to be easier than she'd thought. She probably wouldn't even need to find the rest of the TodaysGirls to sign her petition.

Darryl took the petition, signed it, then handed it to Ryan. "Sign this, lab rat."

Ryan scribbled his name on a line and then looked closer at the other signatures on the petition. "Oh no! My sister is your campaign manager? I should've known you'd pick Miss Perfect to run your campaign."

Maya snatched the petition from Ryan's hands. "Thank you for your support, Ryan," she said as she walked away.

Maya found two more students willing to sign then wandered back to her lab station, the petition complete.

As soon as the bell rang, Maya made a beeline for the office and gave the petition to Mrs. Wertz, the office secretary. Her husband, Walter, was on the faculty at Edgewood Community College with Maya's mom. Maybe that was why Mrs. Wertz always seemed to take a special interest in Maya, Morgan, and their brother, Jacob.

"I'll see that this gets to its proper place," Mrs. Wertz said. "Now you're an official candidate."

Maya beamed. Why hadn't she thought of politics a long time ago? This was going to make a great career. Maya strolled to her locker, basking in the newfound attention, when Bren bounded down the hall.

"Is it true?" Bren squealed. "Are you really running against Camille Bates?"

When Maya nodded, Bren grabbed her shoulders and squealed again. "This is so great! You're going to hammer her in this election. No question about it."

Maya was tempted to agree outright, but she decided on a more modest approach. "Who knows? I'm going to try. That's for sure."

Bren was beside herself. "We need to go to the mall—makeup, clothes, the works. A political fashion statement!"

This is the very best part of running for office, Maya thought. *You even need new clothes and makeup.* "I'm there, Bren. You can be my fashion spin doctor."

That brought Bren up short. "Spin doctor?"

Maya laughed. "It's what politicians call the people who advise them on how to dress, act, behave, react, whatever. You know, put a good 'spin' on something?"

Bren smiled. "OK, 'Doctor' Mickler thinks we need to hit the mall."

On the ride to Edgetowne Mall, Maya explained all about Karen Dean-Malloy and her preference for tailored suits. Knowing that the stores where they usually shopped wouldn't carry suits, they parked Mr. Beep near the main entrance of Lanning's Department Store. Junior dresses were on the second floor, and the store usually had a large selection of suits this time of year.

Maya lingered longingly over a lime green suit made of raw silk.

"Forget it," Bren said behind her. "That is way too hot for the campaign. Let's go check out the navy blue suits."

Maya moaned. "I'm going to end up looking like Mrs. Clark."

"Not quite," Bren said. "Besides, if you want to look more serious than Camille, you've got to buy the right outfit. Like this one."

Bren held up a slim, doubled-breasted suit with classic lapels. The matching skirt was a great length—just short enough to gracefully show off Maya's shapely knees and lower-thighs.

"Oh, yeah," said Maya, growing weak with admiration. "That is *the* suit."

It wasn't until she was styling in front of the three-way mirror in *the* suit that Maya lifted the price tag and looked at it.

"A hundred and twenty dollars!" Maya said out loud. "That's a lot of Gnosh checks."

Bren frowned. "Oh come on, Maya. That suit is marked down from a hundred and eighty. And besides, you look great in it. As your fashion spin doctor, I strongly advise you to buy it. How many suits do you own?"

"None," Maya replied sheepishly. "When would I need a suit? To sling junk food at the Gnosh?"

Bren took a Lanning's charge card from her wallet. Her parents had given it to her for her fourteenth birthday. "Here," she said. "Pay me back when you win the election."

"You mean *if* I win the election," Maya countered, still studying her reflection in the mirror.

Bren snorted. "If you campaign in that suit, it's a done deal."

Maya nodded thoughtfully. If she was going to be a serious candidate, she probably ought to dress like one. Karen Dean-Malloy would approve.

"OK," Maya said. "I'll use your card for a short-term loan. But after the election, I pay you back."

Bren grinned. "Congratulations, Maya. You just won this election."

That evening, the chat room was abuzz with politics.

faithful1: I've got some GR8 ideas 4 the campaign!!!!
nycbutterfly: tell me, oh wise campaign manager!!!!!!!!!

TX2step enters the room

TX2step: Don't tell me, let me guess. nycbutterfly is running 4 president????

nycbutterfly: U R SO close--student council.

chicChick: U should C the kewl suit nycbutterfly bought at the mall.

TX2step: U R going 2 run 4 student council N a swimsuit? Won't U get cold???????

nycbutterfly: U R so hilarious hahahahahahahahahahahahahahaNOT!

faithful1: seriously, can every1 meet at the Gnosh tomorrow nite? We need 2 have our first campaign meeting

chicChick: kewl, I'm there.

jellybean: me 2

TX2step: do campaign workers get free food?

jellybean: AND free sodas!!!!!

TX2step: ok. I'm there

faithful1: what about U, rembrandt?

rembrandt: I work tomorrow nite so I'll serve the eats.

nycbutterfly: can U make cool posters for the campaign? U R the best artist in the school!

rembrandt: if I have time between work & school & watching my sisters faithful1: don't worry, rembrandt. We only need about a dozen posters.

rembrandt: I'll help if I can

nycbutterfly: Kewl, rembrandt. First I need to get more info on the dress code.

TX2step: DRESS CODE???? UR not behind that RU??? That is a totally stupid idea.

nycbutterfly: chill 2step. I just need to get more info on it. Mrs. Clark wants to have a dress code @ school

TX2step: Mrs. Clark is a WALKING dress code

jellybean: hey, not 2 change subject, but do U know Lori Kate Cox?

TX2step: she's a freshman, right?

jellybean: ya. it's sorta weird. After school, she was taping a sign on her locker that said maya cross for student council. how did she know?

nycbutterfly: that is so kewl! don't know how she found out

TX2step: Lookout butterfly. You have a stalker!!!!!

chapter.3

By 6:00 A.M., Maya was up, showered, dressed in her new suit, and writing an e-mail to her newfound role model.

Dear Senator Dean-Malloy,

Inspired by your career in politics, I have entered the race for student council at Edgewood High School. Many students tell me I have a good chance of winning this election. Thank you for being a role model for women in government.

Sincerely,
Maya Cross

She hit *Send*, leaned back in her chair, and stretched luxuriously. The day seemed ripe with possibility. Maya stuck her head into Morgan's room. Her sister was still snuggled under her comforter, fast asleep. At the foot of Morgan's bed, her fat orange tabby cat, Vinnie, dozed contentedly.

"Hey, sleepy," Maya called gently. "Check out my power suit."

Morgan opened one eye, then rose up on one elbow and struggled to open her other eye. "Sweet. You look like that Carry Malley congressperson."

"You mean Senator Karen Dean-Malloy," Maya said, trying to sound annoyed but enjoying the comparison. "Well, maybe a little."

Morgan's alarm clock began buzzing furiously. She reached over, batted the snooze button to silence the alarm, then rolled onto her back with a groan.

"Come on, Morgan," Maya said. "Let's get to school early for a change, OK? This is going to be a busy day for me."

Luckily, Coach Short had a statewide coaches' meeting in Bloomington and had canceled swim practice. The last thing Maya wanted was to get her hair wet or have to redo her makeup. No swim practice gave her a chance to get an early start on the day. She wanted to scout the best locations for her posters and make notes for that night's campaign meeting.

"Move it or lose it, little sister!" said Maya, and fifteen minutes later, Morgan was pulling on the shoulder straps of her overalls as Maya hustled her out the back door. In the car, Maya cringed as she watched Morgan eat a bowl of organic bran flakes. Morgan got several minor soy-milk baths thanks to Mr. Beep's starts and stops between their home and school.

"Serves you right," said Maya. "Of all the days I wanted to be here early—"

Morgan's chin dropped so far it could have landed in her lap. "Maya, look!"

A yellow banner hung over the school's main entry from the student parking lot. Huge red letters clearly spelled out its message: "VOTE 4 BATES."

Maya felt her stomach grab her appendix. Bates? Camille Bates?

Inside, the halls were decorated with posters of every size. Other candidates had used standard poster boards, hand-lettered with markers.

But Camille's were professionally printed on metallic reflective material. One VOTE 4 BATES! sign even had a battery-operated blinking red light for the point in the exclamation mark.

Students were wearing "Vote 4 Bates" campaign badges, and some of Camille's girlfriends wore sashes that had "Bates Babe" written in silver glitter. They buzzed around Camille like fruit flies swarming an overripe banana.

"Unreal," Morgan whispered.

Maya needed to figure out her next move. And fast. "Not to worry," she said, sticking out her chin and trying to sound confident. "Just wait until you see what I have planned for *my* campaign."

Maya marched off to her locker, throwing her shoulders back

and pasting a confident smile across her face. There was no way she would let anyone see how unprepared she felt for this campaign. Especially not Camille Bates.

All through her first-block geometry class, Maya fretted and schemed about how to handle Camille in government class. When the moment came, she waited until just before the tardy bell rang to enter the government classroom, then casually sauntered in, sat down, and gazed serencly around the room.

Mr. Wallace was already at his lectern, arranging his notes. When Maya smiled at him, he beamed back. She was sure he'd tipped that cowboy hat she imagined sitting on his head.

"Well, this is an unexpected pleasure," he drawled. "Right here in this class, we have democracy in action. Camille tells me that we have two political candidates—Camille Bates and Maya Cross—running for the same office. Would you like to kick off your campaigns today?"

Camille stood up as if on cue, her nostrils flaring larger and rounder—"Yes, I'm prepared to discuss every aspect of this campaign. First and foremost, I've given this matter of the dress code a lot of thought. And I can't understand why anyone would want to support a dress code. The students don't want it, and I am voicing the students' concerns. My political team, the Bates Brigade, will get the message out to every voter in the school: we represent you and will stand up for your freedom to wear what you want to wear. Freedom for the students of Edgewood High School!"

The room erupted with clapping and shouts of enthusiasm. Camille's nostrils went pink from the admiration. She grinned and sat down.

This can't be happening, Maya thought desperately. *I feel like I'm in some horrendous dream being chased in slow motion by a monster—Camille—shooting fire out her nostrils!*

"Maya, would you like to make an opening campaign statement?" asked Mr. Wallace.

Summoning a smile, Maya stood up. "I agree that freedom is important. But none of us knows how Mrs. Clark defines dress code. How strict is it? I mean, is she talking about uniforms or simple neatness? Until we know a little more about her plan, I don't think we can fully discuss this issue."

Maya heard a muffled groan and then silence. The class seemed completely uninspired by her response.

"Maya has raised a good point," said Mr. Wallace. "Does anyone know any specifics of the proposed dress code?"

No one raised a hand.

"Well, then perhaps we should hold a debate in class when we've all had a chance to review the specifics of the dress code," said Mr. Wallace. "Would you two be willing to participate in a political debate?"

Camille leaped at the opportunity to speak first. "I'd be happy to debate my opponent on this very important issue."

Mr. Wallace looked at Maya. She felt like he'd just cracked a whip across her forehead. Totally unprepared for the question, she mumbled, "I would also be happy to debate my opponent," even though she wasn't sure where she stood on the issue. Immediately she wished she hadn't said the same exact thing that Camille had said.

But what else could she say? Neither of them knew the specifics of this whole dress code issue. So why did Camille seem so confident while Maya felt blindsided?

She brooded through the rest of class, her thoughts far away from the day's lesson topic. When the bell rang for lunch, Maya had already decided that she would rather starve than spend lunch near Bat-Cave-Bates and her fruit fly posse.

On the way to her locker, Maya saw Amber working her way through the crowded hall, waving frantically.

"Remember the lunchtime candidates' meeting in the principals' office?" Amber said. "The candidates and campaign managers for every class are supposed to attend."

Maya groaned. "Does this mean I get to spend lunch with Camille Bates again?"

"Don't blame me," Amber said. "I told you yesterday we should have moved to another table. Besides, this meeting is supposed to be a short one. And it involves the candidates from every class—not just Camille."

With only a small conference table for seating, most of the candidates and their campaign managers had to stand. Maya and Amber found room near the door.

"Thanks for coming," Mrs. Clark said. "We'll keep this brief because of the cramped meeting space. The campaign officially starts today and will wrap up next Tuesday with the election. Remember, as candidates you are setting an example for other students. I expect you to conduct yourselves with dignity and show respect for other candidates. Anyone who cannot do this will be disqualified. I have a written list of rules to clarify what's expected of you. Any questions?"

Before her nostrils could twitch, Camille's hand shot into the air. Mr. Carson nodded.

"I've got some political ads for my campaign," she said. "Can I use the closed-circuit video system on campus to run my ads?"

Mrs. Clark clicked her ballpoint pen several times before answering. "Certainly, as long as everybody has equal access to the system. We will give everyone the same amount of airtime, and those who want to make a short political speech can do so. Any other questions?"

Again, Camille's hand fluttered in the air. Mrs. Clark gave her a crisp nod.

"What about the school's Web site?" Camille asked. "Can we post our campaign platform on the site?"

Mrs. Clark looked at Amber, who had developed Edgewood High's Web site. "Is that a possibility, Amber? How much work would be involved?"

Amber chewed her lower lip for a moment. "We would need to set up the format for it," she said. "But that shouldn't be too complicated. I think I can have it ready by the end of tomorrow."

Mrs. Clark clasped her hands together. "Splendid. Camille, I think your suggestions will add some gusto to the election."

Maya didn't need to look at Camille to see her smile beaming back at Mrs. Clark.

"Any other questions?" Mrs. Clark continued. "No? All right then, candidates, I want this to be a fair and honorable campaign. Go out there and show us how the political process is supposed to work."

With Mrs. Clark's words echoing in her head, Maya's scrambled to figure out her next move. She already felt so behind. How had she ever gotten sucked into running for office? Who needed this?

Silently, Amber and Maya filed out of the principals' office. Neither of them spoke until the crowd had dispersed and the two of them were alone in the hall.

"OK, here's the plan," said Amber. "After school, we go to the Paper Barn and load up on supplies for making campaign posters. Have no fear—we are going to blow Camille Bates out of the water!"

"Yeah," Maya sneered, doing her best to act invincible. "Right out of the water."

But for the rest of the day, it was Maya who felt like she was drowning. She couldn't keep her mind on French or chemistry. All she could think about was how humiliating it would be to lose to Camille Bates. There had to be some way to build a campaign that was better than Camille's. But how?

Maya got through her afternoon classes and was puttering by in Mr. Beep when Amber walked out of the school's front doors.

"Hey, door-to-door service!" Amber said, tossing her books in the backseat. "I like being the campaign manager."

"Wanna trade places?" Maya said quietly, navigating her way through the crowded parking lot.

Amber looked sharply at her best friend. "This doesn't sound like you, Maya. What's up?"

Maya shrugged wordlessly. Amber opened her mouth to say something but stopped. The two drove toward the paper store in silence.

"What if I—" Maya couldn't finish her thought out loud.

"Lose?" Amber finished the sentence. "So that's what this is. OK, so you lose."

Maya kept her eyes on the road, her hands squeezing the steering wheel in a death grip. "Lose to Camille Bates? That's the most humiliating thing I can think of right now!"

Amber smiled. "There's always that possibility. But doesn't it seem like you're giving up a little too easily? It's only the first day of the campaign."

Maya stopped at a red light and looked at Amber. "You saw Camille today; you heard all that political gobbledegook. I'm almost afraid to go to school tomorrow morning. With my luck, NBC News will be set up on the front lawn of the school, interviewing Camille!"

Amber laughed. "She totally has you psyched out, doesn't she?"

Maya didn't answer.

"Listen," Amber said. "The best candidate isn't always the one who wins the election. But whether you win or lose, there's one thing you offer the voters: the kind of person who's worth following. Whatever happens in the election doesn't really matter if that's your focus."

"Well, all I know is that Camille isn't worth following," Maya said defensively.

"That's true," Amber said. "So if you're a good leader, then you *will* be worth following. But first you need to ask yourself one question: Who do you follow?"

"Why is that important?" Maya asked.

"I read this on Coach's desk calendar," Amber said. "'Don't follow a leader until you know who she's following.'"

Maya pulled up to the entrance of the Paper Barn. In the display window was a campaign poster for Karen Dean-Malloy. Maya pointed at the poster. "Now there's a woman who knows what she's doing. I'll bet Karen Dean-Malloy never doubts herself. If I'm going to survive this campaign—no, if I'm going to *win* this campaign—I've got to be more like Karen Dean-Malloy!"

Amber smiled. "Now there's the fighting spirit I know and love. Come on. Let's go buy a ton of poster board and get this campaign show on the road!"

A set of five neon-color poster paints, wide-tip markers, and a stack of poster-sized cardboard came to $27.50. Maya paid for the materials and kept the sales receipt.

"We're supposed to file a campaign expense report," Maya explained to Amber. "Mr. Wallace said he would give both of us extra credit if we do. You know, democracy in action!"

The girls laughed. It was starting to feel like fun again. On the way to Amber's house, they talked about the campaign and the upcoming strategy session at the Gnosh Pit. Maya pulled into Amber's driveway. "Thanks for the pep talk," she said. "I really needed it."

"No problem," said Amber. "See you at the Gnosh at 7:30."

The afternoon seemed sunnier now than it had right after school. Maya drove through the tree-lined neighborhoods—red, yellow, and orange with fall leaves.

There weren't any cars in the driveway when Maya arrived home. Her parents must still be at work. Maya's older brother Jacob would be at football practice, and who knew where Morgan was. Maya left the art supplies in Mr. Beep and headed for what she hoped would be a completely quiet house. Having the house all to herself was such a luxury.

Maya opened the back door and listened. Not a sound. *Yesssssss!* She practically floated upstairs to check her e-mail. After a quick boot-up, the computer's electronic voice intoned: "You've got mail."

There it was, amid a sea of e-mail advertisements, forwarded jokes, and notes from friends: a real e-mail message from Karen Dean-Malloy!

Maya grabbed the mouse and rapid-fire clicked on the mail icon. Up came the message:

Dear Ms. Cross,

It was so good to receive your e-mail and to know you share my enthusiasm for public service. You sound like you're brimming with confidence and leadership ability. We need more capable women like you in our local, state, and federal governments.

You must be feeling very confident about your election to the Edgewood High School Student Council. Please keep me informed. I look forward to hearing about your landslide victory.

Sincerely,
Karen Dean-Malloy

Maya sat back, panic slowly seeping into her muscles. What had she been thinking when she wrote that cocky note? Why had she sounded so sure of victory? Camille's super-charged campaign was in full swing, and Maya was trying to catch up. If she lost this election, she would look like a complete fool!

"Now I have no choice," Maya said out loud. "I have to win."

chapter.4

Maya heard someone in the kitchen. "Morgan is that you"

"Be right up," called Morgan.

Maya listened to her sister romp up the stairs till she stood in the doorway, chomping on an ice cream bar.

"Did you see the note from Mom?" Morgan asked between bites. "It says she's picking Jacob up after football practice. They're going to the mall to buy a dress shirt for the football banquet."

"Well, that's just great," Maya said flatly. "I'm fighting for my political life, and Mom's at the mall with Jacob."

"So anyway," Morgan continued, "Mom said to eat a healthy snack after school."

Maya eyed the ice cream bar that Morgan had almost

completely devoured. "Is that your idea of a healthy snack?" Maya asked. "Although I don't know what difference it makes to me. Camille Bates is going to eat me for lunch on election day."

Morgan stopped crunching on the chocolate-covered ice cream bar. "What is with you, Maya?" she mumbled. "So Camille put up some big signs and got her campaign going today. So what? I thought you wanted to be like that woman who's running for office. You know, that woman with the two last names."

"Karen Dean-Malloy," Maya said wearily.

"Whatever," Morgan replied. "She seems pretty smart, from what you've said. Maybe she can give you some ideas on how to win this election."

Maya was about to resume whining when she stopped and thought about what Morgan had just said. Maybe her sister was right. Hadn't Karen Dean-Malloy just sent her an encouraging e-mail? If anyone could give her some ideas for beating Camille Bates, the Honorable Senator from Indiana, Karen Dean-Malloy, certainly could.

"You know, Morgan?" Maya said as she typed the senator's Web address into the computer browser. "Sometimes you're so good, you're even cooler than me!"

"Funny," Morgan said around the ice cream in her mouth. She swallowed and smiled. "I think I saw a story in this magazine about her family. She has kids and a husband . . ."

But Maya's fingers were already flying over the keys, typing in search words that would bring information about Sen. Dean-Malloy.

The search turned up a list of articles from several magazines. In *Washington Insider* magazine, there was a photo spread titled "Best Dressed on Capitol Hill." There was a picture of Dean-Malloy, featuring the senator at a state dinner for some visiting dignitaries.

She was wearing a fitted black evening gown, and her hair was swept up in a classy chignon. She was engaged in conversation with Vice President Hurston and Congressional Speaker of the House Neal Hooks, both dressed very elegantly in black tie. Maya thought the whole affair looked *tres chic.*

The next periodical was the *Washingtonian Monthly.* Last spring, the magazine had done a feature spread on Dean-Malloy's family. Posed on a brocade sofa in the family's Georgetown home were the senator, her husband, and their two children. The article said Ron Malloy worked for an environmental political action committee in Washington. He was every bit as handsome and polished-looking as the senator.

The couple's children were now teenagers. Jason, their son, was fourteen, and their daughter, Hedy, was seventeen. The article said that both children were students at St. Albans, an exclusive boarding school in suburban Washington, D.C., that attracted many politicians' children.

"The family makes a special point of getting together once a month for a family outing," the article read. "Previous outings have included long weekends to ski in Vermont and enjoy the sun in the Florida Keys."

That last sentence made Maya swoon. Imagine jet-setting to Vermont or Florida for the weekend! Weekends at the Cross household usually consisted of housecleaning, laundry, and late-night cleanups at the Gnosh Pit. How glamorous was that?

Studying the photo of the Malloy family, Maya thought that Jason and Hedy looked content, surrounded by all of that Washington wealth and privilege. They must be so proud of their parents' high-profile jobs.

Maya saw one more periodical listing that interested her. The *Washington Post* had photos of government officials under the headline "What's Wrong with This Picture?"

One photo showed Karen Dean-Malloy driving a pricey-looking sports utility vehicle. The caption read "Enviro-friendly Karen Dean-Malloy Driving Enviro-UN-friendly SUV." The paragraph below explained that although Dean-Malloy had been elected on a platform of preserving the environment, the SUV she drove had one of the worst gas-mileage ratings of all the models being sold today; it was clearly bad for the environment.

This makes no sense, Maya thought. *She drives a VW Beetle, just like me. Her e-mail was very clear on that.* Maybe this sports utility vehicle was a rental car, Maya reasoned. Or maybe it was the car she drove in Washington, and she kept her VW Bug in Indiana.

There's only one way to find out, Maya decided. She closed the window she was reading and clicked over to the Karen Dean-Malloy Web site. She double-clicked on the Environmental Issues button and a video clip began playing. It was of Dean-Malloy, standing at a speaker's podium, delivering an impassioned plea for more environmental regulations.

"My friends, we've got to stop wasting our natural resources," she said. "I pledge this as my ceaseless goal—to make the automobiles of this country more fuel efficient. We'll tell the auto companies, both foreign and domestic, to make their gas hogs fuel efficient or take them off the American market!"

The way Dean-Malloy said the phrase "I pledge this as my ceaseless goal" gave Maya goose bumps of admiration. She decided to download the sound bite to her desktop and use that phrase in a campaign speech.

"You've got mail," the Instant Message voice said. Maya quickly clicked over to the IM window. There was a message from Amber:

time 2 leave for the gnosh pit. don't be L8 2 your own campaign committee meeting!!!!!

Maya typed in "thanx!!!!!" and quit the IM program. She glanced at her bedside clock: 7:20. *Rats!* No time to change clothes, and she had been in her suit all day. *This must be what it feels like to be on the campaign trail,* Maya mused.

Maya found Morgan at the kitchen breakfast bar, doing her biology homework. "Hey, let's hit it, Morgan," Maya said, grabbing her purse and car keys from the countertop. "We're gonna be late for the campaign meeting!"

Morgan began turning out the lights.

"Forget the lights," Maya yelled. "Let's get outta here!"

The sisters were out the door and in the car before Camille Bates could have twitched a nostril. Maya backed out of the driveway and raced Mr. Beep as though the little Volkswagen were an Italian sports car.

"Mom's gonna give us her 'turn out the lights' speech when we get home," Morgan said, holding on to the dashboard with one hand and the armrest with the other as the tiny car zoomed through town.

"I'll take the blame for the lights," Maya fumed. "Like it's going to break the bank if we leave a few lights on."

Morgan kept her eyes on the road, wincing when Maya drove too close to the curb or the bumper of the car in front of them. "I don't think it's the money as much as it is wasting energy," Morgan said. "You know how important that is to Mom."

Maya roared up to a stoplight, stood on the brakes, and looked at Morgan. "Hey, I'm the politician here, remember? I know all about environmental issues."

Wednesday nights at the Gnosh Pit were always lively. It was youth league night at the Bowl-A-Rama, and teams often met at the Gnosh before and after games for hamburgers.

Coach Short was there with his three sons, Harrison Jr., Nat, and Chris.

"Mo-gun!" the little boys squealed when Morgan entered the restaurant. Morgan sprinted to the table where Coach and his sons ate ice-cream sundaes. Pre-schooler Chris had more chocolate syrup on his face and hands than his sundae did. Somehow Morgan managed to hug him without coating herself with the sticky goo.

Maya watched her sister with an equal mix of admiration and disgust; admiration for the enthusiastic way Morgan connected with kids and disgust for every child's perpetually gooey state of personal hygiene.

Jamie bustled between the kitchen and her tables while Amber sat in the big round booth in back. Amber waved hello and called to Maya, "Hey, what's up!"

"Where is everybody?" Maya asked as she slid into the booth.

"If you mean Bren, I don't know," Amber said. "She's the only person who's always later than you are. When she gets here, we can start the meeting."

Jamie came over to the girls' table. "Your dad said to tell him when the meeting started, so he could send over a free pitcher of Mountain Dew and your choice of snacks. So what'll it be?"

Maya was taken aback. "Aren't you going to join us? I know Dad wouldn't mind waiting tables for a while."

Jamie seemed hesitant. "Look at this crowd," she said. "I

can't sit down and shoot the breeze while the place is this busy. It wouldn't be fair to your dad."

Mr. Cross was at the cash register, ringing up customers' bills and taking to-go orders on the phone. He looked over, saw Maya, grinned, and gave her a wink.

Maya scooted out of the booth and made her way through the crowded restaurant. She waited until her dad finished taking a to-go order and hung up.

"Yes, ma'am," Dad said in his official teasing voice.

"Is it OK if Jamie joins us for our campaign meeting?" Maya asked. "I don't want her to feel left out."

Dad shrugged his shoulders. "I tried to tell Jamie that I would give her a paid break so she could help you girls organize the campaign. She wouldn't hear it. Jamie said I wasn't paying her to sit around and chat with her friends. That girl is a hard worker. She's going to be a big success someday."

Maya shook her head. Jamie was not only a loyal friend but also probably the hardest worker at the Gnosh. "Thanks Dad," Maya said, hugging her dad. "At least you tried."

Maya went back to the big booth where Jamie was putting silverware and napkins around the table. "Maybe when things die down a little you can join us?" Maya asked Jamie.

"Maybe," Jamie said. "If I can . . ."

Morgan and Alex slid into the booth. "Look who I found," said Morgan. "Alex is gonna help, too."

Alex's expression looked like she had a mouthful of Limburger cheese—and wasn't enjoying it.

"Thanks," said Maya, wondering how her sister had convinced Alex to come. "Alex, I'm sure your help will be invaluable."

Alex grunted.

Jamie returned with a pitcher of Mountain Dew and some clear plastic tumblers filled with ice. "Is six glasses enough?"

"Better get a few more," Amber said. "Take a look."

Maya followed Amber's gaze to the entrance. Morgan's friend Jared headed toward their table. And behind him, Bren came through the front door with Bobby McClain on one arm and Todd Green on the other arm. She looked like a homecoming queen without the tiara.

"Is this campaign headquarters?" Bren called to the group. "I have some volunteer workers for the campaign."

"What campaign?" Bobby asked. "I thought we were volunteering to eat burgers with you tonight."

Bren giggled. "You are so funny! I told you we need to come up with ideas on how to get Maya elected to student council. Right, Todd?"

"Whatever," Todd replied, his eyes scanning the room. Maya's eyes met Amber's and the two exchanged looks of exasperation. Not exactly the level of enthusiasm they were looking for in campaign workers.

"OK, let's get started," Amber said, adopting a businesslike tone. "As you all noticed today at school, Camille Bates has launched her campaign big-time. Banners, badges for students, the works. And she's already written campaign ads for the school's video system and Web site. So we have a lot of work to do just to catch up with Camille. We need to come up with a better campaign. Does anyone have any ideas?"

"I do," said an unfamiliar voice. Maya turned and saw a short, wiry girl with ash blond hair standing next to the booth. She was dressed in a navy blue, pinstriped power suit and a short hairdo that was an uncanny duplicate of Maya's hairstyle.

"Lori Kate Cox," she said, reaching out to shake Maya's hand while balancing a stack of files and notebooks in her other arm. Maya shook her hand, mildly amused at Lori Kate's go-get-'em attitude.

"Morgan told me you were meeting tonight," she continued in her brisk, no-nonsense style. "Sorry I'm late, but I had some research to do at the library."

"Research?" Maya echoed, looking puzzled. "What kind of research?"

Now it was Lori Kate's turn to look puzzled. "For the campaign, of course. I think we have a good chance of winning this election. If we do a few things right. Would you like me to explain?"

Maya looked at Amber, who shrugged and smiled.

"Go for it, Lori Kate," Maya said. "This should be interesting."

chapter.5

"Observe!" Lori Kate said, directing her laser pointer to the first line of a chart she had placed in one of the Gnosh's two wooden highchairs. The chart held a list of items Lori Kate had written in red marker under the words: MAYA STRATEGIES.

"Item number one," Lori Kate continued. "Be PRO-Active instead of RE-Active. Do not let your opponent define who you are to the voters. Instead, define yourself who you are and what your issues are."

"I'm not sure I follow this," Bren said. "Say that again."

"OK," Lori Kate said, clicking off her laser pointer. "Camille Bates wants to be the candidate who represents the students. We can't let her be that. We have to portray Maya as the candidate who represents the students. I'll give you an example. Camille says she's against the dress code. Where do we stand on the dress code?"

"I like the idea of a dress code," Bren said. "Unless it would force us to wear some ugly uniform."

"Dress codes are stupid," Alex said. "How can we let the administration tell us what to wear? What about our rights?"

Lori Kate looked at Maya expectantly.

"It . . . it's more complicated than that," Maya stammered. "We don't even know what Mrs. Clark is proposing. So how can we know if we're against it?"

Alex groaned. "Any dress code is too much. I think Camille Bates is right. A dress code stinks."

Alex's comments stung Maya. "Camille is just saying that to get elected," Maya snapped. "Once she's in office, Camille is off the hook. If you vote for me, I'll make sure the dress code allows casual clothing like baggy pants and flannel shirts. And that's a more honest answer than you'll get from Camille Bates."

Alex seemed unconvinced. "Why should I believe you?"

Lori Kate snapped her fingers and lit up like a neon sign. "That's it! That's the campaign theme: honesty!"

Amber picked up on Lori Kate's theme. "Honesty, Maya for Honesty," Amber murmured. "Or what about this: Maya Cross: The Honest Choice."

"Maya Cross: The Honest Choice," Maya repeated. "I like it."

Bren nodded enthusiastically. "I can get T-shirts printed

with that slogan. And have a bunch of the guys at school wear them. You know, like walking billboards! Would you do that, Todd?"

"Sure," said Todd, swallowing a large gulp of Mountain Dew. "Is the food ready yet?"

Bren smiled apologetically to the group. "Todd's a growing boy with a big appetite."

"Then I'm just in time," said Jamie, presenting a tray of cheeseburgers. People scrambled to move their sodas to make room. "Dig in! Compliments of Mr. Cross."

"Cool, Maya," Todd said, hefting a monster half-pound burger. "Your dad's pretty cool."

"Hey, Jamie," Maya called. "What do you think of the campaign slogan 'Maya Cross: The Honest Choice'?"

Jamie shrugged. "It's OK."

Maya was slightly wounded. "Just OK?"

Jamie looked uncomfortable. "Well, like what does it mean?"

Lori Kate pounded her fist on the table. "Honesty, that's what it means! Maya is the honest candidate. Who wouldn't vote for an honest candidate? We have to drum that into the voters' heads: honesty, honesty, honesty!"

Jamie shrugged. "I guess I'm just not into politics."

Jared timidly waved his hand. "Can I make a suggestion? I heard one of Camille's friends saying that she's a great humanitarian because she wants to get students involved in Toys for Tots. Can we think of something like that for Maya's campaign?"

"Great idea," Morgan said, reaching to bonk fists with Jared. "What can we do, Maya?"

Maya was stumped. "I don't know. This whole campaign thing has happened so quickly. I really never thought about needing a humanitarian cause. Looks like I'm in trouble on that one."

"I beg to differ," Lori Kate said, handing Maya a photocopy of the school paper from Maya's freshman year. Maya scanned the article: "Ned Potter and Maya Cross have announced plans to form a local chapter of Habitat for Humanity. Potter and Cross have completed the paperwork to join the national organization and the co-founders say they plan to hold an organizational meeting in the next few months."

"What happened to the local chapter?" Lori Kate asked.

Maya winced. "Ned and I couldn't decide who should be president. We both wanted the job. So that was the end of the local chapter. We never even held the first meeting."

Jared laughed. "Well, that clears up that mystery. A couple of my friends and I talked to Coach about forming a local chapter of Habitat. We wrote to the national headquarters. They wrote back and said that Edgewood High School already had a local chapter, but they gave us permission to start our building project."

Maya was confused. "So how does this help me or my campaign?"

"I bet the national organization lists you as president of the local chapter," Jared said. "Our group is meeting tomorrow night to discuss our building project. You can come and find out about our house, and even pitch in this weekend."

Maya forced an enthusiastic smile at the news. "Great, Jared. I think Habitat is an awesome cause!"

"Then we all agree," said Lori Kate, as if she were suddenly in charge of the campaign. "All of us should show up tomorrow night. We can even take pictures of Maya working on the house this weekend."

Amber nodded. "Good strategy, Lori Kate. Now if Bren can be in charge of the campaign T-shirts, and Jamie can help us with some posters—"

"Excuse me," Lori Kate cut in. "I have some ideas for posters here in my notebook. I can also make some posters with our new slogan: Maya Cross: The Honest Choice."

"That would be great," Amber said. "Maya and I can work on the campaign ad for the school's Web site. Anything else?"

"Yeah," Todd said, jumping into the conversation. "Is anybody going to eat the rest of that burger?"

Amber and Maya gave each other exasperated looks. "It's all yours, Todd."

Todd grabbed the last half of Maya's burger. "Hey, look at me, Bren," he said, ripping the burger in half and taking a big chomp out of each piece. "Two-fisted feeding frenzy!"

Even Bren rolled her eyes at that remark. *Where does Bren find these meatheads?* Maya wondered.

"Thanks for coming to tonight's meeting and for all your

good ideas," Amber said to the group. "It sounds like we have the right strategy to win this election: Maya Cross: The Honest Choice!"

Bren stood up and linked arms with Todd and Bobby. "Gotta run. See ya!"

Jared, Morgan, and Alex edged their way out of the booth and meandered over to Coach Short's table. With the meeting officially adjourned, Maya was left sitting in the booth with Amber and Lori Kate.

"Thanks a lot for your help," Maya said.

Lori Kate shrugged and gathered her notebooks and charts. "See you at the Habitat house tomorrow night."

"OK," Maya said, mustering some enthusiasm. "Do you need a ride home?"

Lori Kate acted as though Maya had just offered her a million dollars. "Oh thanks, that's so nice! My mother will be here any minute. But thank you. I mean, thanks a lot."

Maya nodded and smiled. "You're welcome. See you tomorrow."

Amber and Maya watched as Lori Kate walked purposefully out the front door. Without a word, they began stacking the plates and tumblers.

"OK, I give up," Maya said, breaking the silence. "Why is Lori Kate working on my campaign?"

"Because she admires you," Amber replied. "What other reason could there be? She's young and energetic, and she likes politics."

Maya considered Amber's response. "Maybe. But why was

she wearing a suit like mine? And her hair was almost identical. What is that about?"

Amber grinned. "Imitation is the sincerest flattery. I guess it all depends on whether you are the imitator or the imitated."

"What's that supposed to mean?" Maya asked.

Amber laughed. "Well, you certainly don't mind imitating Karen Dean-Malloy. But it makes you nervous when Lori Kate imitates you. What's the difference?"

Maya thought for a moment. "I don't know. I guess it's easier to be a follower than a leader. Being in the spotlight is scary. If you mess up, everybody knows it."

"Just be someone worth following," Amber said. "Then you can't mess it up."

Later, Maya and Morgan drove most of the way home in silence.

"Maya?"

"Yeah?"

"Are you really going to the meeting at the Habitat house tomorrow night?"

Thursday night was the only night of the week that Maya and Morgan set aside to watch TV. Their favorite TV drama, *Upper East Side,* was on at 8:00. They camped out on the sofa, ate popcorn, and watched the cast of good-looking, well-to-do New Yorkers live out their triumphs and tragedies. Giving up even one episode of *Upper East Side* felt like a huge sacrifice.

"I really don't have much choice," Maya said. "Remember, I need to come across as some big humanitarian."

Morgan nodded in sympathy. "Yeah, I know. Jared really wants me to help with the Habitat project too."

As soon as the girls walked in the back door of their house, they could hear the sounds of their parents talking over the television in the den. Mom and Dad were lounging on the sofa, their feet propped on the well-worn coffee table.

"I really don't care for that woman," Maya heard Mom say as she entered the den.

Maya's eyes traveled to the TV screen. There was Karen Dean-Malloy, elegantly dressed in a burgundy wool suit, fielding questions from a panel of reporters. Mom's words landed like a karate kick in Maya's gut.

chapter.6

"How can you say that? Karen Dean-Malloy is my role model!"

Maya felt wounded and insulted at the same time.

Mom picked up the TV remote and turned down the volume. "Don't get me wrong, Maya. I like to see women in important jobs, particularly African-American women. But she seems to say one thing and do another. Haven't you noticed that?"

Maya realized that, other than the sound bites she had heard on TV and the Web site, she really didn't know where Dean-Malloy stood on most issues. But she certainly wasn't going to admit that to her mom.

"Well, uh, she sent a personal e-mail to me," Maya stammered. "And she drives a Volkswagen because they're more fuel-efficient than big cars."

Mom smiled. "You drive a Volkswagen, too. And I'd be willing to bet that you drive your Volkswagen more as your primary transportation than she drives hers."

Maya was incredulous. How could Mom make fun of Dean-Malloy? Maya looked at her dad for support, but he laughed and waved his hands in mock surrender.

"I'm not getting in this argument," he said, grinning. "After a whole day at the Gnosh, I think I'm entitled to some quiet veg-out time. You two can discuss politics without me."

Maya turned back to Mom. "I'm going to do some more research on Karen Dean-Malloy. Then I think you'll have a different opinion about her."

"That would be great," Mom said. "I love to talk politics. Especially with my daughter. We need to know more about our leaders—what they stand for, why they choose the cars they drive."

It was downright scary the way Mom could turn Maya's challenge into an invitation for political discussion. Mom took the art of discussion seriously and was very well read and articulate. She made Camille Bates look like a pushover in comparison.

"OK, you're on," Maya said. "But can we do this later? I need to check my e-mail. First things first!"

Mom picked up a small pillow and pretended to throw it at Maya's head. Maya squealed and ran out of the room and up the stairs. As soon as she was in her bedroom, she shed her suit, pulled on her flannel pajama bottoms and matching tank top, and flipped on her computer. The girls' Web site,

TodaysGirls.com, filled the screen, and there was Amber's Thought for the Day:

> **Send me your light and truth. They will guide me. Lead me to your holy mountain. Lead me to where you live. --Psalm 43:3**

What had Amber said about being someone worth following? *Easier said than done*, Maya thought. *It's hard to be a leader when everyone expects different things from you.*

The nightly chat session was in full swing when Maya entered the chat room.

> **chicChick:** tell the truth. who's the real hottie . . . todd or bobby?
>
> **TX2step:** the 1 with his mouth stuffed with burgers!
>
> **chicChick:** that would B Todd?
>
> **TX2step:** dunno . . . all muscleheads look the same 2 me.
>
> **nycbutterfly:** well r'nt u precious, TX?
>
> **TX2step:** no problem, your candidate-ness--or whatever we're supposed 2 call U now
>
> **nycbutterfly:** i'm 2 tired 2 think about the election
>
> **rembrandt:** I can have some posters ready for 2morrow.
>
> **nycbutterfly:** thanx, rembrandt, i need 2 get my name around school
>
> **TX2step:** the clone should B able to do that!

chicChick: where did she come from?

TX2step: a parallel universe

faithful1: she seems like a nice person and we need help!

jellybean: she's working hard 2

TX2step: yeah and she eats less than Todd!

chicChick: LOL--not!!!!! Todd is KEWL

rembrandt: i'm sleepy and i need 2 start on posters. CYAL8R.

nycbutterfly: g-nite rembrandt! thanx again . . .

jellybean: i'm tired 2. nite all

TX2step: i'm outta here. butterfly, don't 4get to read
    Lori Kate a bedtime story 2nite!

nycbutterfly: how's this 4 a bedtime story: TX2 goes 2
    sleep and stops bugging princess candidate!

TX2step: no way. who'd believe that?

Maya left the chat room and considered turning off her computer. But instead, she typed in the Karen Dean-Malloy Web site address. In a moment, she saw an image of the senator, looking as stylish as ever, and a list of her accomplishments trailing down the page. She seemed to be so in control, so sure of herself, so full of integrity.

"Please be real," Maya said quietly to the senator's smiling photo. "I need you to be real."

chapter.7

Maya was up early the next morning. The first item on her morning's agenda was to select her outfit. Although she truly did appreciate the effort Lori Kate had gone to, it still bugged Maya that Lori Kate had this quirky urge to dress exactly like her. Maybe it was just a one-time thing, she reasoned.

Instead of wearing her Karen Dean-Malloy suit, Maya selected a very different look: a tan faux-suede miniskirt and a blue chambray shirt over a white tank top. No way would Lori Kate show up in the same outfit. Maya even changed her hairstyle, wearing it down and slightly curled under. *Let her try to copy this*, she thought.

The halls were still empty when Maya arrived at school. The first thing that caught her eye was a large sheet of poster board hanging in the student center. The poster read: "You can't lead someone to the light if you're standing in the dark. Maya Cross: The Honest Choice!"

Maya tried to hide her astonishment. The poster was huge, the lettering was neat and crisp, and the message was . . . Maya reread the poster with a growing sense of exhilaration. The poster implied that Camille Bates was standing in the dark! How edgy can you get? Jamie was one incredible poster artist!

Down the hall, near the cafeteria, was another mammoth sign. This one read: "Before following a leader, see if she's headed in the right direction. Maya Cross: The Honest Choice."

Maya laughed out loud. This one was clever because it was complimentary to Maya while casting doubts on Camille's ability to know the right direction.

"Where did this poster come from?" Amber was standing beside Maya, reading the sign overhead.

"Jamie, I guess," Maya said, grinning.

Amber didn't seem as enthusiastic. "That surprises me. Jamie usually doesn't take cheap shots like that."

"Cheap shots?" Maya echoed. "I think they're very creative. And they make you stop and think."

Amber didn't respond, and Maya didn't press the point. But it seemed ungracious not to appreciate the time and effort that went into making the large posters.

"Oh, here are some badges I made for the campaign." Amber grabbed a handful of the paper circles she had cut out and lettered with the new slogan. They weren't nearly as fancy as the ones Camille Bates was distributing. But Maya felt grateful that Amber had made them in such a short time.

"Thanks!" Maya said, pinning the paper circle on her shirt. "You're the best."

Maya saw Jamie down by her locker and waved to her as Jamie shut the locker door. Jamie joined the girls under the large poster.

"These large posters are fantastic!" Maya said. "You really outdid yourself on them."

Jamie peered at the writing on the poster. "I didn't make that poster. I drew the ones that have a swirling Day-Glo color pattern and say, 'Vote 4 Maya.' I put them up in the halls near the pool and the cafeteria."

"Oh yeah," Maya said, pretending she had seen them. In fact, the only posters she had noticed were the two mammoth signs with the edgy comments. Maya made a mental note to look for Jamie's. "Thanks," she said. "I know how tired you were last night. I really appreciate it."

Jamie smiled. "No problem. Well, I'm off to class. See ya."

"Wait a minute," Amber said. "Here comes Lori Kate."

Lori Kate, sporting the same hairstyle and navy suit she had worn yesterday, walked toward the group, "Good morning," she called out. "Why aren't you wearing your suit, Maya?"

Maya shrugged. "I spent too much time in it yesterday," she said.

"Oh," said Lori Kate. "Well, you've got to play the part. So, how do you like the posters?"

"You made them?" Amber asked.

Lori Kate nodded. "I sure did. What do you think?"

Maya laughed. "I love them. They're so edgy! You must have worked on them all night!"

Lori Kate gave a modest shrug, but it was obvious she enjoyed the praise. "I took the quotes from several different reference books in the library and sketched them out on the poster board. Last night I just added our new campaign slogan: Maya Cross: The Honest Choice."

"Awesome!" Maya said, bonking fists with Lori Kate.

"One more thing." Lori Kate reached into her book bag and brought out a bag of professional-looking campaign badges with the new slogan emblazoned on them. "I'm having another 150 made up today. My sister in middle school has a badge maker, and I'm paying her to make them for me."

"Thanks," Maya said, pinning the badge on the other side of her chambray shirt. "How much do I owe you for these? I want to pay you for them."

Lori Kate smiled. "No need. My dad bought a crate of these blank badges from a salvage store. Now my sister has enough badges to elect the next ten mayors of Edgewood. And I told her that I would do all of her chores for the next two weeks if she would make these for me."

Lori Kate gave badges to Amber and Jamie, then began pinning one on her own lapel. The bell for first block started ringing.

"See you at lunch, OK?" Maya said to Lori Kate, who nodded and scurried down the hall. Maya looked back at Amber, who said nothing.

"I don't get it," Maya said. "I really don't get it. Why is she doing this for me?"

Amber shook her head. "I don't know. I guess I'm a little confused. And embarrassed, too. For what it's worth, you don't have to wear that dorky paper badge I made."

Maya wanted to drop her books right there in the hall and give Amber a big bear hug. "Don't be silly," Maya said gently. "I know how much work goes into making these things. You are my best bud in the universe, remember? Come on, let's get to class before we get a pink slip."

Students who were late for class got sent to the attendance office and were given a pink tardy slip. A bouquet of five pink slips equaled one detention.

"OK, universal best bud," Amber said with a grin. "See you in government class."

Maya daydreamed through most of geometry, trying to appear interested in congruent polygrams.

Her thoughts were fixed on the election, her friends, and why Lori Kate was expending so much energy on her. Mercifully, the bell finally rang, and she could drop the pretense of being thoughtfully engaged in whatever the teacher was saying.

She was still pondering the election when she dropped her books on her desk in government class and eased into her seat.

Maya's eyes traveled around the room, watching students collapse into their chairs, settling in before starting a conversation with another student nearby. She saw Jamie walk into the room, and they exchanged smiles.

Maya's gaze was still idly wandering around the classroom when her eyes met Camille Bates's. Those steely eyes were staring back with such venom that it made Maya's heart jump. Camille's nostrils warmed to a deep scarlet and pulsed once before she turned away. Her expression said she had seen something so disgusting she couldn't bear to view it a second longer.

Maya felt stunned by Camille's reaction. What had happened to the Little Miss Sugar act Camille worked so hard to promote?

As Mr. Wallace handed back the graded the papers they had turned in last week, his boots tapped and shuffled across the tile floor. "I want to commend you all for the amount of work you obviously put into these papers," he said as he neared the bottom of the stack.

He stopped in front of Camille's desk and thumbed through the last few. "So how's the election campaign?"

Camille sat upright in her seat—her nostrils had cooled to a pale pink. "Well, to be perfectly honest, I've been the victim of some extremely negative campaign posters. My opponent's trashing me to make herself look better."

Every head in the class turned toward Maya and all the little noises stopped.

"That's quite an accusation," Mr. Wallace said, and Maya

knew he meant, "Them's fightin' words." "Would you explain what you mean?" he asked Camille.

"I'd be happy to," Camille answered, already warming to the spotlight. "There's a poster that says, 'You can't lead someone to the light if you're standing in the dark.' As if I'm standing in the dark! That's a negative campaign, and it's from a candidate who'd rather trash me than talk about the issues."

Maya didn't want to take Camille's bait in front of the whole class. "As a matter of fact, that quote is about leadership," Maya said evenly. "I think it's a very insightful comment. That poster doesn't mention you by name, does it?"

"It doesn't need to mention my name," Camille shot back— her nostrils were Tabasco red now and quivered with seismic anger. "Everyone knows who you meant. I should've known you'd try to pull some dirty tricks in this election!"

"Oh really?" Maya said. "I think it's pathetic to trash me so everybody will feel sorry for you. Talk about dirty tricks!"

"Excuse me," Mr. Wallace interrupted the showdown. "We need to keep this discussion on the level of political discourse, not a talk show brawl."

Camille gave Mr. Wallace a soulful look. "You're absolutely right, Mr. Wallace. I want to run a completely honorable campaign. I think the students of this school deserve an elected representative with high moral character."

Maya wanted to groan out loud. Camille Bates was positively shameless when it came to buttering up adults. The rest of the block, Maya ignored Camille and tried to seem nonchalant about the blowup between them. When the bell rang, she purposefully fussed over her books and reorganized the contents of her backpack until the room had emptied.

Bren and Amber had gone on ahead, but Jamie was waiting for her by the door.

Maya hoisted the strap of her backpack over her shoulder, finally ready to go. The girls headed toward the cafeteria in the now-empty halls.

"Camille really pounced on you, didn't she?" Jamie said. "She's one tough cookie."

Maya nodded. "Yeah, but I'm starting to see how she works. Yesterday I was sure I was going to lose the election. But now I think I can beat her at her own game."

Jamie and Maya went through the cafeteria line, then found Bren, Alex, Amber, and Morgan seated in their usual spot.

Alex took a large swig of root beer and wiped her mouth on her sleeve. "I think those big posters are totally cool. What did that one say? 'Before following a leader, see if she's headed in the right direction.' It sounds like a giant fortune cookie! I'm starting to enjoy this election."

"That's more than Camille Bates can say," Maya replied. "She took my head off in government class—accused me of trashing her by saying she was in the dark."

Amber looked uncomfortable. "Well, isn't that what we said?"

"Oh, come on," Maya said. "I think that quote is pretty harmless."

"I think it's funny," Alex said. "And a lot more entertaining than most of the boring election signs around here. No, wait! Look who just walked into the cafeteria."

The girls followed Alex's gaze, and Bren gasped. There was Lori Kate, wearing a short tan skirt, tank top, and blue shirt—as close to Maya's outfit as she could manage. She had even changed her hairstyle, brushed down and curled under. Somehow, between the beginning of school and now, Lori Kate had transformed herself, once again, into a mini-Maya.

"OK, I'm putting a stop to this," Maya said, irritation seeping into her voice. "This clone thing has gone right off the edge."

Lori Kate waved a folded paper frantically at Maya and squeezed her way through the lunchtime crowd of students. Maya steeled herself for Lori Kate's next weird surprise.

"Lori Kate, we need to talk," Maya began.

"We sure do," Lori Kate gasped, almost out of breath. "Read this!"

She held up the front page of *The Eagle's Nest*, Edgewood High's newspaper. The boldface headline blared out the announcement: *"Nest Endorses Bates."*

chapter.8

*H*ow *could this happen?"*

The girls huddled around the newest edition of *The Eagle's Nest*. The headline on page one was a stunner: "*Nest* Endorses Bates."

"How could this happen?" Amber repeated.

"I think it's pretty obvious," Lori Kate said. "Bethany Troyer's the editor. Guess who Camille's campaign manager is?"

"Unbelievable," Bren said, crunching on a celery stick. "Can they get away with this?"

"They can if we let them," Maya said. "But we're not going to let them."

After listening to Camille whine about honorable campaigns, Maya was livid—Camille had used her friend's job to snag an endorsement.

"The campaign rules say 'all school-supported venues must give equal time or space to all candidates,'" Amber said, reading from the paper that had been passed out at the candidates' meeting in the principals' office. "That means the closed-circuit TV system, the school Web site, and the school newspaper. This is a clear case of cheating."

Maya folded the newspaper and stood up. "It's time for a visit to Mrs. Clark."

"Do you want us to come along for support?" Amber asked.

Maya considered the offer briefly. "Thanks, but I think I want to talk to her one-on-one. If we all storm in there, it might look like we're ganging up on Camille. After all the garbage I took from Camille in government class, this is pay-back time."

Mrs. Clark usually ate lunch at her desk, so finding her was easy. Maya knocked gently on the open door. Mrs. Clark was on the phone but motioned Maya to come in.

"Certainly, I'll hold," Mrs. Clark said into the receiver. She looked up. "Hello, Maya. What's up?"

"I need to talk to you," Maya said, handing the newspaper to Mrs. Clark.

"Have a seat," Mrs. Clark said. "I'm on hold with the state board of education."

Maya lounged in the seat, trying to look nonchalant while secretly stealing glances at Mrs. Clark's face. As Mrs. Clark read the headline and following story, Maya could discern some displeasure, then a stony expression.

"Thank you, Maya," Mrs. Clark said in her chilly, heads-will-roll voice. "I appreciate you sharing this with me."

That was Maya's cue to leave. "Thanks, Mrs. Clark. Bye." She waited until she was alone in the hall to do a small, shoulder-wiggling victory dance. *Camille Bates thinks she can mess with me? I don't think so!*

After school, Maya found Amber in a small room off the computer lab where she updated the school's official Web site. Maya told Amber about her short but productive meeting with Mrs. Clark.

"Girl, you should have seen the look on her face when she read that article," Maya said.

Amber grinned, a fellow conspirator. "Sorry I missed it. Especially after all of that business about running such an honorable campaign. Which reminds me: I've worked up some ideas for an advertisement to put on the school Web site. It isn't as edgy as Lori Kate's posters, but it won't get us in trouble, either. Want to see what I've got so far?"

Amber clicked into the school's Web site. She was about to click into a document titled "Maya Campaign Ad" when Maya stopped her.

"Hold on, what's that?" Maya pointed at the screen. A document at the bottom of the screen was titled "CB Election."

"I'm guessing it's Camille Bates's election ad that'll run on the Web site," Amber said.

Both girls were silent, thinking about what juicy information might be contained in that document. They exchanged looks and smiled.

"It's tempting," Maya said.

"It is tempting," Amber agreed.

"She would never know that we read it," Maya said.

"That's true," Amber said.

"And she certainly hasn't been playing fair with us," Maya added.

"No, she hasn't," Amber agreed.

The two sat quietly, weighing the options.

"OK," Maya said impatiently. "As much as it kills me to say this, maybe we should do the right thing and leave it alone."

Amber nodded and smiled. "I knew I was campaign manager for the right candidate."

The next day, a new edition of *The Eagle's Nest* came out, complete with a front-page retraction of Camille's endorsement.

"I regret the unfortunate error I made in endorsing a candidate for student council," the retraction read. "As campaign manger for the endorsed candidate, I deeply regret my error in judgment. The candidate herself had no prior knowledge of the endorsement and should not be blamed for the error. I have recused myself as editor of the newspaper until after the election." The short article was signed "Bethany Troyer, Editor."

"What does *recuse* mean?" Morgan asked out loud. She and Maya were in Mr. Beep on their way home from school.

"It's the same as ex-cuse," Maya said. "When judges have a conflict of interest in a legal case, and they take themselves off the case, they recuse themselves."

"Wow," Morgan said in hushed awe. "That sounds serious."

"It is," Maya said, feeling perky and upbeat. This whole incident had turned into a major embarrassment for Camille's campaign.

"So are you going to be at the Habitat meeting tonight?" Morgan asked.

"Of course," Maya replied. "Just as soon as I figure out what to wear."

Morgan frowned. "Don't get too dressed up, Maya. Everyone else will be in jeans and sweatshirts."

Maya gave her sister a patient, exasperated sigh. "Like I don't know how to dress? You just leave the fashion decisions to me."

"And don't forget to be there by 7:30," Morgan said. "Coach starts those meetings on time. I'm going early with Jared, so I won't be at home to remind you."

"Oh, woe is me!" Maya said, her voice filled with sarcasm. "My baby sister won't be here to run my life for me. What shall I ever do?"

"Be late as usual," Morgan mumbled.

Maya pretended that she hadn't heard the remark.

As soon as she got home, Maya checked her e-mail. An e-mail from Karen Dean-Malloy turned out to be a group message announcing that the senator would be interviewed on network news that night.

Maya had more than enough time to select an outfit for the Habitat meeting before the interview. A quick scan of her closet produced nothing. Overalls seemed like a good choice, but the only pair she owned were made of black velvet. Way too dressy, Maya decided. Chinos? More like it, but maybe too summery. She flopped on her bed and thumbed through a stack of fashion magazines. One advertisement showed a woman at a construction site, posed on a steel beam and dressed in a glittery evening gown and a hard hat. *Forget it,* Maya thought, tossing the magazine on the bed.

The late afternoon shadows made Maya feel drowsy. *I'll just close my eyes for a quick nap,* she told herself. When she awakened, the room was dark and she could hear the TV downstairs. Maya sat up and looked at her alarm clock. 6:35 P.M.

"No way," Maya said aloud and yawned. She had been asleep for almost two hours.

Maya wandered downstairs. Mom looked up from the stove. "I wondered where you were, sleepyhead," she said. "Dinner'll be ready in less than five minutes."

Mom usually insisted that the TV be turned off during dinner. But Maya told her about Dean-Malloy's interview on the evening news and she relented. The family, minus Morgan, was about halfway through Mom's four-cheese tortellini when the news anchor said, "Next: Feeding the Hungry. A new generation of legislators."

The video clip showed Karen Dean-Malloy talking to homeless people standing in line at a soup kitchen.

"This is it!" Maya squealed. "There she is—my role model."

"If she's helping feed the homeless," Dad said, "she's my role model, too."

"I can't argue with that," agreed Mom.

After the commercial break, the news report began. "In downtown Indianapolis, the homeless and the hungry have found a hot meal at the New Pathways Soup Kitchen. And yesterday, Senator Karen Dean-Malloy was there to roll up her sleeves and give the gift of food as well as a check from the Model Cities program, a federally funded program to help feed the homeless."

The video clip showed the senator parking her Lexus SUV in a tow-away zone and greeting destitute-looking people in a line outside the soup kitchen. As usual, she was dressed stylishly in a power suit with velvet lapels.

"I hope she's not planning on serving any soup in that outfit," Mom said dryly. "That suit had to cost at least $1,000."

"Yeah." Dad laughed. "I can't remember the last time I wore a suit to work at the Gnosh Pit."

There they go again, Maya fumed silently, *making fun of my hero.* When the report finished, Maya glanced at the clock and realized she needed to leave in about ten minutes to get to the Habitat meeting on time.

"Gotta go," she said, standing up and carrying her plate to the counter. She dashed upstairs and looked in her closet. It was hopeless. Nothing to wear and no good ideas. She grabbed her navy blue suit and quickly pulled on the skirt and jacket. She pushed at her hair a few times in front of the mirror and pulled on some sling-backed heels.

"Bye," she called as she rushed past her parents, who were still eating and watching the news.

"Slow down, Maya!" her dad called as the back door slammed shut.

Gotta be on time, Maya told herself as she drove across town. She got behind an old rusted Dodge Charger that crawled along at 20 miles an hour. *Come on, come on*, she repeated, drumming her fingernails on the steering wheel. *Drive or get off the road!*

When she arrived at the Habitat house, Maya groaned. There had to be two dozen cars parked along the street and driveway. She crept around the block, trying to find a reasonably close parking space.

This is ridiculous, Maya fumed. *I'll be out here all night!* There was a small space in front of the house, but when Maya pulled up alongside to parallel park, she saw a fire hydrant near the curb.

"Too bad," she grumbled, parking the Volkswagen in the small space. "Anyway, it's dark, and no one cares."

When she burst into the living room, the meeting was already in progress.

"We have a lot left to do, so we're gonna have work sessions on Friday *and* Saturday this week. You're gonna get dirty this weekend," Coach said, "so leave your nice clothes at home."

Maya found a seat near Amber, Morgan, Jamie, and Lori Kate.

"Jamie has offered to videotape our work this weekend," Coach said. "We thought it'd be good to show others what we do and how we do it."

Maya leaned over and whispered to Jamie, "Great idea, Jamie."

"It was Coach's idea," she whispered back.

Lori Kate leaned over to Maya. "Wouldn't that be great for our campaign ad? Your face on videotape, the humble humanitarian?"

The video camera in Maya's mind was already rolling. She saw herself in a sharp burgundy suit, standing amid the construction bustle, delivering a Dean-Malloy–type speech that would stir people's hearts to action. Years from now, people would still remember her speech, and it would live on through the ages. Her introduction had a familiar Dean-Malloy ring to it: "My fellow students, the students of Edgewood High need a strong voice. I am that voice. Vote for Maya Cross!"

chapter.9

When Maya's thoughts wandered back to the present, Coach was droning on about construction committees, deadlines, and cost considerations.

Like I care about this stuff, Maya thought, checking her watch, looking around the room, and bouncing her knee. *How much longer can Coach talk about these details? When does the fun start?*

"Now, who has experience with power tools?" Coach asked. "Can I see a show of hands?"

Maya raised her hand. She looked around and saw Morgan giving her a look of surprise.

"I use a Dustbuster in my bedroom!" Maya shot back under her breath. Jared rolled his eyes at her, and his shoulders shook with laughter.

OK, that's it, Maya decided. She grabbed her purse and, scrunching down, made her way to the back of the room and out the door. When she reached Mr. Beep, there was a piece of paper under the windshield wiper. Maya snagged it, got in Mr. Beep, and turned on the dome light.

"No way!" Maya wailed. "City of Edgewood, Police Department, Traffic Violations? Parking next to a fire hydrant!"

Now she had to scrape up money for the fine. Maya stuffed the ticket into Mr. Beep's tiny glove box and cranked the ignition. As she sped homeward, Maya comforted herself with a generous dose of self-pity. *I wasn't in there a half-hour. It's a conspiracy to discredit me. Camille Bates probably called the police station.* OK, that one seemed outlandish, even to Maya. But it felt good to blame someone else for that stupid ticket.

When Maya walked into the kitchen, Mom and Dad were sitting at the breakfast bar going over the books from the Gnosh Pit.

"Another good month," Dad said. "With this extra profit, I think I might go ahead and buy a better ice machine. Hey, there's Princess number one. Where's Princess number two?"

"Still at the Habitat house," Maya said. "I couldn't take it any longer. The whole meeting was Coach standing up and talking. But I did get a great idea for my campaign."

Maya explained the idea of videotaping her volunteer efforts and using it as a campaign video.

"Just like our senator," Dad said. "You're welcome to use our

77

new camera for the taping. Just be sure to charge the battery for at least three hours before you use it."

"Maybe some of your campaign video should include your thoughts on leadership," Mom said. "I think the voters should know what kind of leader you'll be. I just read a good quote about that in a teaching journal: 'Education can't make us leaders—but it can teach us which leader to follow.'"

Leave it to Mom to get all intellectual about this. On the other hand, Maya did appreciate the way Mom was always so supportive of her dreams.

"OK," Maya said. "I'll try to write down some ideas about being a leader."

After shedding her suit for pajamas, Maya checked her e-mail. A message from Karen Dean-Malloy turned out to be another group e-mail, thanking her supporters. There was also a complaint about media coverage. "The videotape on the network news, showing me parked in an illegal parking space, is yet another example of the media's deliberate attempts to discredit me with voters," the e-mail read.

"I'm down with that," Maya said, remembering her own problems with Edgewood High's media.

"You've got mail," the mailbox signal flashed on her screen.

Maya double-clicked on the new mail icon, and a message from Lori Kate appeared:

Dear Maya,
    Love the idea of your campaign videotape! What are
you wearing tomorrow night to Habitat? Gotta go!
                        Lori Kate

Maya laughed. There was no way she would tell "Copy" Kate
what she was wearing for the Habitat videotaping. Not unless she
was dying to see Lori Kate in the same outfit. Which she wasn't!

Maya heard the back door close then Morgan talking to their
parents. Soon after, Morgan plodded up the stairs. She opened
Maya's door and stuck her head inside.

"Chat room at nine," Morgan said.

"OK, thanks," Maya replied. She clicked into the
TodaysGirls.com Web site and read Amber's Thought for the Day:

**Be humble and give more honor to others than to your-
selves. Do not be interested only in your own life, but
be interested in the lives of others. --Philippians 2:3–4**

**Good leaders care about the people who follow them.
That's what makes them good leaders!**

Jamie had posted one of the campaign designs in the Artist's
Corner. "Vote for Maya" was written in a swirling font that
caught the eye and was easy to read. Jamie always made it look

so easy, combining just the right lettering with subtly shaded color—a born artist with a strong desire to create beautiful things.

Maya signed on and soon the girls were awash in conversation.

faithful1: wait til U C the campaign platform I'm writing. We get a full page in the Eagles Nest on Monday, and I want 2 B ready!!!!

nycbutterfly: KEWL! what does it say?

faithful1: it sez the admin should let students dress comfortably but neatly

rembrandt: does that mean I can still wear Levis??????

nycbutterfly: of course!!!

faithful1: we have 2 have a strong platform so Camille doesn't make it sound like we're against the students.

nycbutterfly: thanx, faithful1. hey can U guys run the video cameras 2morrow at Habitat?

rembrandt: sorry i'm working @ gnosh pit 2morrow

jellybean: TX and I can film, right?

TX2step: WRONG

nycbutterfly: Y not?

TX2step: i know what'll happen. U'll B way way bossy!!!

Alex could be such a pain. But Maya needed everybody's help on this campaign. Summoning all of her diplomacy, Maya responded.

nycbutterfly: i promise 2 be extra nice! PLEEEEEEZ?

TX2step: OK, i just wanted U 2 beg me!!! hehehehe

chicChick: what R U wearing 2morrow?

nycbutterfly: funny U should ask! i got an e-mail from Copy Kate! she asked what i was wearing. like i'm gonna tell HER?

TX2step: Copy Kate? 2 cool!

chicChick: she wants 2 help, but Copy Kate is 2 much . . .

rembrandt: promised baby sis a bedtime story. CUL8R!

Maya signed off, shut down the computer, and climbed into bed. So far, the campaign was on track. With all of her friends helping, she was feeling pretty confident.

Morgan and Maya were actually early for swim practice the next morning when they saw the new mint-green mini-posters. The notebook paper-size posters featured a yearbook photo of Camille with the caption: "Camille Bates—Leadership we DON'T need!"

Maya's eyes met Morgan's, and they both said the name out loud: "Copy Kate!"

The girls grabbed the posters off the walls and stuffed them into a recycling bin.

"Hey!" Maya looked down the hall and saw Amber running toward her, hands full of the mint-green posters.

"Has that girl lost her mind?" Amber said, gasping for breath.

"I don't know," Maya stammered. "This is just so weird . . ."

"Are there any more posters still up?" Morgan asked, joining them in the hall.

"I don't know," Amber said. "I got all the ones in the hall by the office. If Mrs. Clark sees these, she'll be furious!"

Maya's mind was reeling. "OK, I'll take the science wing, and Morgan, you take the hall by the band room. Let's see, what's left?"

"The library and the language lab halls," Amber replied. "And I can check the computer lab on my way."

"Great!" Like a football huddle breaking, the three girls ran off in opposite directions. Of all days to come to school early, Maya was especially glad they had today. Of course, this would mean they'd be late to swim practice, but Maya would rather face an angry Coach than an angry Mrs. Clark. If only they could get to all the posters before anyone else saw them.

Upstairs in the science hall, Maya could hardly believe what she saw. There was Lori Kate, slowly tearing off pieces of masking tape and placing the posters on the wall. Maya ran up to her, and Lori Kate grinned. Maya tore down the poster Lori Kate had just taped to the wall.

"Are you crazy?" Maya sputtered. "Do you want to get me thrown out of this election?"

Lori Kate seemed genuinely puzzled. "I thought you liked the edgy stuff," she said. "This leaflet idea was all mine."

Maya didn't know where to begin. "Look, I know your heart is in the right place, but this kind of sign will make the voters hate me. No one likes negative campaigning. Saying good things about me is fine, but trashing Camille will only help her and hurt me. You can understand that, can't you?"

"Sure," Lori Kate said, grinning. "I know exactly what you mean. Hey, I hope I didn't cause you any trouble with this."

Maya smiled patiently. "Let's just hope that Mrs. Clark hasn't seen any of these. And that Camille Bates didn't come to school early today."

"OK." Lori Kate nodded, still grinning. "See you tonight for the videotaping at the Habitat house."

"Sure," Maya said. She watched Lori Kate walk down the hall and turn the corner. Maya glanced at the hall clock and sighed. What a way to start the school day . . .

Maya found Morgan and Amber in the library.

"Lori Kate was in the science wing," Maya said. "She was putting up posters as fast as we were tearing them down."

The girls laughed.

"We had a little chat," Maya added. "I think she understands now."

"Coach is gonna be furious," Morgan said.

"I'll talk to him," Maya said. "I think he'll appreciate what we did. If not, at least he'll be mad at me and not you. Let's get going."

On their way to practice, Maya saw Jamie and grabbed her arm.

"Hey, I need you to make some more posters," Maya said.

"That Lori Kate almost got me in a ton of trouble today with hers. I need the new ones for tonight."

"Tonight?" Jamie said between gritted teeth. "I'm working tonight! And I'm working tomorrow if your dad needs me. And I'm watching Jordan and Jessica for my mom tomorrow night. You can't just order up more posters. I'm not a printing press!"

chapter.10

Maya was still reeling from Jamie's response. "I've never seen her that angry," she told Amber. The girls were setting up an online digital connection from the school's closed-circuit TV system to the Habitat site.

"Look at it from her side," Amber said. "Jamie's completely overwhelmed. She's trying to work at the Gnosh and get good grades and help her mom with baby-sitting Jordan and Jessica while Mrs. Chandler finishes law school. And Jamie did make all of those artsy posters for your campaign. I think she's just exhausted."

"Yeah," Maya agreed. "I guess my timing stunk." Maya made a mental note to e-mail an apology to Jamie. She knew that a face-to-face apology would be too intense for her shy friend. But an e-mail would be perfect.

"So explain this to me one more time," Maya said. "How does this digital connection thing work?"

"It's really pretty simple," Amber said. "All we need is a laptop that can pull up the school site. Then the cameras just feed into the laptop and *voila,* it's live coverage—but we'll edit it later for the campaign advertisement."

Maya shook her head in wonder. Amber was so capable when it came to computers and how the systems connected to each other.

"I'll be there to coordinate the taping," Amber said. "I can get Alex and Morgan to set up their cameras and then make sure the digital feed is working. I just hope we don't get in everybody's way while we're trying to do this."

"What do you think I should wear?" Maya asked.

"A flannel shirt and overalls?" Amber suggested. "Something that looks realistic."

Maya tried to look enthusiastic. A flannel shirt was not exactly what she had envisioned, but she wanted this to go well and help the campaign. "I've got overalls. Maybe I can borrow a flannel shirt from Morgan."

Amber smiled. "Just be there early so I can get the taping done early. I'm not sure how long the volunteers are going to want to work around the video cameras."

"No problem," Maya said. "I'll be more than ready."

At 6:00 P.M., Maya stood in front of her full-length mirror, dressed in her black velvet overalls and Morgan's red and black plaid flannel shirt.

Not my first choice, Maya said to herself. But not entirely bad, either.

Maya had just sat down to write an e-mail to Jamie when a message from her popped up:

Maya,
    Sorry i got so steamed at U 2day. Lost my KEWL entirely!!!!!
                         Jamie

What a great friend! Maya hit *Reply* and typed:

Jamie,
    U will always be KEWL with me. Sorry I was so demanding. I know how hard UR working. The posters U made are way cool and more than enuf for the election. thanks for all your help.
                         Maya

Maya hit *Send* and watched her message disappear into cyberspace.

She clicked the newsgroups icon. There was a story about Karen Dean-Malloy with the headline "Negative Campaign

Ads." With another double click, Maya brought up the story on the screen.

> Senator Karen Dean-Malloy charged today that negative news leaks from challenger Rodney Gorman are "not about political issues but amount to personal attacks." Sources from the Gorman campaign insist they did not leak misleading information to an Associated Press reporter concerning Dean-Malloy's ties to several large industries accused of polluting air and water in the greater Indianapolis area.

Maya felt herself getting angry at the injustice of the Gorman camp's tactics. And she shuddered to think what might have happened if she and Morgan hadn't discovered those mint-green leaflets smearing Camille. She shut down her computer, stretched, and stood up. Might as well get to the Habitat house a little early, she reasoned.

Mom was in the kitchen, arranging a fruit platter. Several faculty members were coming over for an informal meeting to review plans for a new project. Bowls of salsa and chips were already on the table with a lush green tabouli salad and a wicker basket of kaiser rolls.

"Bye, Mom," Maya said as she pulled on her coat and headed for the back door.

"Aren't you having dinner?" Mom asked. "Wait a minute. At least take a granola bar and some fruit to eat on the way. I thought you weren't leaving for another hour."

"I need to be early tonight," Maya insisted. "I don't have time to eat."

But Mom had that look on her face. "Let me fix you a sandwich," she said. She packed a cracked wheat roll with tuna salad—Maya's favorite.

Mom put the sandwich on a plastic plate and heaped some blue corn chips on the side. "Here," she said, handing the plate to Maya. "And take this juice with you. You need something nutritious if you're going work all evening."

There was no arguing with Mom when she had her mind made up. Maya took the full plate and bottle of cran-grape juice. "Thanks, Mom. See you tonight."

Unfortunately, Mr. Beep had been manufactured in the early 1970s, well before the age of built-in beverage holders in cars. Maya stuffed the juice bottle between her knees and balanced the plate on her lap. This arrangement would make shifting gears difficult, but at least she would have both hands free to drive.

Usually, waiting for a red light was interminable. But Maya used the time she spent waiting at each red light to chomp bites out of her tuna sandwich. She ate the chips while speeding along the neighborhood streets and swallowed gulps of juice at the stop signs.

Maya's meal on wheels was going nicely until the stop sign on Mulberry, where she reached for the juice bottle. Looking down, she saw a large glob of mayonnaise-coated tuna swimming down the front of her black velvet overalls.

"Aaaaagh!" Maya screeched. She pulled Mr. Beep to the curb and threw the car into neutral. Placing the bottle of juice on the floor, Maya searched the small car for a napkin or paper towel. Nothing.

In desperation, she lifted the overalls bib to her lips and tried to lick the soupy-looking tuna spill off. But the mayonnaise-saturated spill had already seeped into the fabric.

"I look like a complete slob!" Maya wailed out loud.

If she turned around and went home to change clothes, they wouldn't have time to get the filming in and everybody would be furious. She would just have to find a paper towel and some water to clean up at the Habitat house.

Maya put the juice bottle firmly between her knees and took off for the Habitat house. When she turned onto the block, it was already jammed with cars. "I guess I'll have to park on the next block," Maya said to herself. Just then, Maya felt the bottle shift, and she squeezed her knees together to stop it. Instead, the bottle toppled toward her, and she felt her overalls soaking up almost a half bottle of chilled cranberry-grape juice.

As the icy juice found its way to her skin, Maya tried to leap upward, out of the seat, but in a driver's seat the size of Mr. Beep's, there was nowhere to go. She glanced around in a panic.

The only open parking space was the one in front of the fire hydrant. All she could think about was getting away from the cranberry-grape puddle in her seat.

While arching up out of the driver's seat, she roared into the parking space, threw the car into first, turned off the engine, and leaped out.

She saw Morgan standing on the front porch with Alex.

"Look at me!" she wailed.

"Maya? What's wrong?" Morgan put down the video camera she was holding and ran to the car. Maya stood on the lawn bowlegged, like a cowboy without a horse.

"I am totally soaked with juice, and I've got tuna salad on my overalls," Maya whined. "I can't make a videotape looking like this!"

Morgan's face was an evolving expression of sympathy, amazement, and disbelief.

"Let's go inside and find some towels," Morgan said. "There's no time to go home now."

Morgan helped Maya totter soggy-legged into the house. They found a bathroom with some clean shop towels and a roll of paper towels.

"Will this help?" Morgan asked sorrowfully.

"It's wonderful," Maya said. "Anything to sop up this juice. Thanks, baby sis. I owe you big-time. I'd give you a big hug, but . . ."

Maya looked down at her clothes and then at Morgan.

"Pass," Morgan said, stepping backward and wrinkling her nose at Maya's outfit. *I must be pathetic*, Maya thought. *Even a person who baby-sits gooey small children doesn't want to touch me.*

Morgan left the bathroom, and Maya blotted much of the juice out of her overalls. She even dabbed at the tuna smear, making it look slightly better. *I wonder if Karen Dean-Malloy has ever had a campaign night like this.*

"All right folks, it's a little early, but there are enough of us here to get started," Coach said outside the bathroom.

Maya pulled herself up straight and looked in the mirror. "I've looked a whole lot better," she said. "But at least I'm not late."

"Let's mix up a vat of this taping mud," Coach said as Maya joined the group. "Maya, why don't you help Jared get this ready for our dry-wall finishers?"

Maya looked over and saw Alex and Morgan with their cameras rolling. "Oh, I would love to help!" Maya exclaimed a little too loudly. "I really care about people, especially homeless people!"

Jared added powder to a large tub of water to make the mud mixture dry wallers use with tape to seal the dry-wall seams. "Here," Jared said. "Just stir this paddle around while I pour in the powder. That way we won't have any lumps."

Maya turned to face the cameras. "Why, that is a good idea, Jared!" Maya said in an even louder voice. "This is just like mixing pancake batter for the homeless. And I care deeply about homeless people."

Maya took the paddle and began to stir the mixture. Morgan

and Alex moved closer with their cameras, until they were standing in front of Maya and Jared. The mixture began to thicken, and Maya stirred harder until she heard a small snapping noise. She looked down to see the nail of her left ring finger, completely broken off.

"My nail!" Maya wailed, dropping the paddle. "I broke my nail!"

"Vote for Maya Cross," Alex said in a mock-serious documentary voice. "She cares about the homeless. And her manicured nails!"

Maya glared at the camera. "Is the sound turned on?" Maya said, suddenly forgetting her broken nail. "'Cuz it better not be . . ."

"Vote for Maya Cross," Alex repeated in the same mock-serious tone. "She is a Great Humanitarian who cares about the homeless and her fingernails. But she doesn't like camerawomen very much."

Maya shot Alex a steamed look. "How would you like me to come over there and shove that camera down your ratty throat?"

Alex began shaking the camera. "Now the camerawoman is quivering with fear because the Great Humanitarian wants to shove the camera down her throat. Please don't hurt me, Great Humanitarian!"

But Maya wasn't listening to Alex anymore. She was staring in amazement at the door. Alex slowly panned her camera to the doorway. There stood Lori Kate, dressed in black denim overalls and a flannel shirt.

"Well, how about that?" Alex said in the documentary voice.

"We have a special guest on tonight's show. The Great Humanitarian's biggest fan, Copy Kate, is dressed just like her. Except that Copy Kate's clothes don't look exactly the same. Copy Kate's clothes aren't covered with tuna and grape juice!"

Maya stared at Lori Kate's outfit, then down at her food-stained clothes, and back at Lori Kate. This was one humiliation too many. Maya grabbed her car keys and strode imperiously past Lori Kate into the evening's darkness. It wasn't until she had opened the door of her car and sat down with a squish that she remembered the puddle of juice still waiting for her.

chapter.11

It took Maya a full thirty seconds after waking up Saturday morning to remember that she had promised to spend the day working at the Habitat house. As the memory of last night came flooding over her, the sun-lit morning lost its cozy warmth.

Arriving home last night, Maya had drowned her sorrows in a welcoming hot shower, followed by a pampering succession of lotions and powders. She had even had the presence of mind to clean Mr. Beep and throw her soggy clothes into the washing machine (on the cold-water, gentle-wash setting: thank goodness for washable velvet!).

But now, cuddled under her down comforter, Maya faced the prospect of spending a whole Saturday at the Habitat house. And that scenario only made her want to burrow deeper into the covers and never get out of bed again.

The delightful smell of pancakes and sausage wafted up the stairwell and found Maya under her comforter. She could hear the clattering, sizzling sounds of cooking, and the smells soon became irresistible. Throwing on a pink fuzzy bathrobe, Maya wandered downstairs and climbed onto a stool at the breakfast bar.

"There's my future senator," Dad joked as he flipped a line of pancakes on the griddle. "How are you this morning? And how many of these cakes do you want?"

"Two, please." Maya yawned, and then thought about Dad's first question. "I've been better. I can't wait for this stupid election to be over."

Dad served up two fluffy pancakes and put the plate in front of her. "You picked a tough career. There's no pleasing everybody. And when you're an elected official, everybody's your boss."

"There's a cheery thought," Maya said. "Are those turkey sausages?"

"They sure are," Dad said, picking up two sausages with kitchen tongs and placing them on Maya's plate. "Can't you hear them gobbling?"

"Please, Dad." Maya groaned. "I don't want to picture them in little Pilgrim hats while I'm eating."

Dad laughed. "Fair enough. So what are you up to today?"

Maya found herself telling him all about the grape juice spill, the disastrous videotaping episode, and Lori Kate showing up in the same outfit. "The thought of going back there today just about makes my skin crawl."

Dad listened, looked sympathetic, and nodded. "I feel for you, Maya. A lot of kids would just stay in bed and forget the whole thing. But you remind me of your mother. She's a strong person with a gentle soul. And she never quits when the going gets tough. What does that little sign on her desk say? 'A real leader faces the music even when she doesn't like the tune.'"

Maya nodded. "Well this election tune's getting really old. Karen Dean-Malloy makes her job look so glamorous. So far, this has been a little bit of glamour and a lot of misery."

Dad smiled. "Maybe by the end of this, you'll know whether this politician job is the career for you. Uh-oh, I think I hear another pancake customer approaching . . ."

Jacob wandered into the kitchen, still in his flannel pajama bottoms and Edgewood Football T-shirt, and flopped onto the stool next to Maya. As she listened to Dad and Jacob discuss football strategies, Maya slowly ate her pancakes and let her mind drift far away from the coming events of the day.

Before long, Morgan joined the group downstairs, and Dad dished up another plate of pancakes.

"I told Coach we'd be at the Habitat house by one o'clock," Morgan said between bites. "He said we needed to get a lot done today, or we won't make our deadline. We want the family to be able to move into their new house by Thanksgiving."

"That's three weeks away!" Maya said. "There's no way that house will be ready by then!"

"We're closer than you think," Morgan said. "The dry wall is finished. Coach said we can start painting in some rooms today."

After the election on Tuesday, I am so done with that whole Habitat thing, Maya told herself. She wouldn't be stuck doing it now, except that Lori Kate had thought it was such a great idea. And speaking of Lori Kate, the idea of seeing that copycat show up in her outfit again this afternoon was almost more than Maya could stand. "Who all's working at Habitat today?"

"You, me, Amber, and Alex," Morgan said. "Jared said he'd be there later, after he finishes helping his dad clean out the garage. I think Lori Kate said she couldn't be there today."

That was the best news Maya had heard all morning. After the girls had eaten and dressed, they got Mom's video camera and drove Mr. Beep to pick up Amber and Alex. There was even enough room for Mr. Beep in front of the Habitat house, although his back end did stick out just a little into the driveway.

Inside, the air smelled of fresh latex paint. Coach was assigning each painting team a room. "OK, Maya, your team can paint the smallest bedroom," he said. "Here is your paint, rollers, and trays."

Amber and Maya grabbed the heavy paint buckets. Alex and Morgan shifted their cameras and helped to carry the rollers and trays. The girls set out the trays and filled them with paint. Amber stood on a stepladder to paint the ceiling edges and corners with a brush. Maya stayed on the floor and rolled paint on the flat surfaces. Alex and Morgan readied their video cameras and soon the whole process was in motion.

Maya rolled out a large W of fresh paint on the wall. "Are you getting this?"

"Wait a minute," Alex said. "I see a flashing green bulb in the viewfinder. That means there isn't enough light in here for this camera."

The girls all groaned in unison. "I knew it was too good to be true," Amber said. "We need to find another light bulb for that ceiling fixture. That should make it bright enough to film in here."

"I'll do it," Maya said, putting the roller back in the tray. "Be right back."

Maya searched the house for an extra light bulb. In the basement, a work team of students were rolling block filler onto the cinder block walls. One of the work team was Raj Chowdhury, Maya's friend from French class.

"Hey, Maya," Raj called. "How's the campaign?"

"You don't want to know," Maya replied. "It's a lot harder to run for office than it looks."

Maya told him about Lori Kate and the identical outfits. Then she explained about the videotaping fiasco last night, leaving out the grape juice and tuna salad details. "Hey, do you know if there are any extra light bulbs?" Maya added. "We're trying to videotape some painting upstairs, and the lighting is too dim for the camera."

Raj pointed toward a set of storage shelves. "You should be able to find one over there."

"Maya?" said a voice behind her as she reached for a bulb. Maya turned around, but she already knew it was Coach. And he didn't sound happy. "May I have a word with you?" he said in the same tone.

Maya followed him up the basement stairs, her heart beating louder with each step. Coach walked outside, and Maya followed directly behind him, closing the door behind her. He put his hands on his hips and fixed her with a fierce look.

"For the past week, I've been watching you goof off," Coach ranted. "You've not only been wasting your own time, but you've also been distracting other students who came here to work. You missed swim practice twice last week and were late on Friday. And today I find you down in the basement, socializing instead of helping your team get the painting done. What have you got to say for yourself?"

Maya opened her mouth to defend herself and then stopped. What could she say that didn't sound completely ridiculous? *The only reason I'm here is to make a video for my political campaign? I couldn't find a light bulb so I started chatting with Raj? I spilled a bottle of grape juice on my pants?*

She felt foolish, embarrassed, and dangerously close to tears. "I'm sorry, Coach." Maya said it so softly the sound almost blew away in the autumn breeze. She couldn't think of anything else to add.

Coach appeared taken aback by Maya's reply. "Yeah, well, I appreciate that you're sorry."

Maya nodded, her eyes on the ground. "I really am."

Coach seemed calmed somewhat by Maya's response. "I know how hard you train on the swim team. You've never been a slacker. And maybe that's why I expect more from you. 'Unto those whom much has been given, much will be expected.' Do you understand what I mean by that?"

Maya nodded grimly.

Coach managed a half smile. "When your team is finished with that room, you can call it a day. I just want you to remember what we talked about."

"I will," Maya said quietly.

Coach went back into the house while Maya stood on the front porch, fighting back the torrent of misery rushing through her. She had the strongest urge to walk down the steps of the Habitat house and just keep walking until all of Edgewood was far behind her and she didn't recognize one person, one house, one blade of grass.

The videotape, the campaign, the election—it all seemed like such a huge waste of time and effort—and for what? So Maya could get yelled at by her favorite coach for letting him down?

It took all of her willpower to do it, but Maya went back into the house and found Alex, Morgan, and Amber painting. "Here's the light bulb," she said quietly. "Let's finish this painting."

"Is everything OK?" Amber asked. "You seem a little upset."

"I'm OK," Maya said, too mortified to tell them what had happened. "I've got a headache. Let's finish up here, drop off the video equipment at school, and go home."

The girls finished the painting and cleaned out their rollers, trays, and brushes in the basement laundry sink. Then they got their cameras and jackets and went out to the car. A police officer was standing beside Mr. Beep, writing a ticket.

"This your car?" the officer asked.

"Yes, sir, he is, I mean, it is," Maya said. "What did I do wrong?"

"You're blocking this driveway," the officer said.

"Where?" Maya asked.

The officer pointed to the back bumper of Mr. Beep. The car was partially blocking the driveway, even though there were no cars in the driveway. "We got a complaint," the officer said. "A Miss Brittany Mertz called and said she couldn't back out of the driveway because it was blocked by a blue Volkswagen."

The girls looked at each other in disbelief.

"Brittany Mertz?" Morgan said. "Isn't she one of Camille's campaign workers?"

"I don't believe this!" Maya said. "That is really dirty pool!"

The officer handed the ticket to Maya. "Sorry, miss. Try to stay out of people's driveways when you park."

Maya got into the car and stuffed the ticket into the glove box. She fired up Mr. Beep while Alex, Morgan, and Amber crammed into the little Beetle. Maya drove to the high school, grumbling all the way.

As Maya was parking Mr. Beep, Amber said, "Uh-oh. Look who's here."

Maya looked over and saw Lori Kate getting into her parents' car. *Thank heavens she's leaving,* Maya thought. *I don't think I could handle any more surprises today.* And surprises always seemed to come with Lori Kate.

The school was a beehive of activity. Cheerleaders were practicing in the student center and the wrestling team was in the gymnasium. As the official Webmaster of Edgewood High School, Amber had a key to the Web site room.

"I need to check the monitor to make sure our equipment picked up the video feed," Amber said, pressing a series of keys. The monitor screen filled with a picture of Maya frantically waving her fingers and whining, "My nail! I broke my nail!"

Alex and Morgan giggled softly.

Amber touched Maya's arm. "We can edit that part out."

Amber fast-forwarded the tape and hit play. There was Maya, glaring into the camera. "Is the sound turned on?" Maya was saying in a threatening voice. "'Cuz it better *not* be!"

Alex and Morgan burst into laughter. "Look at you Maya," Morgan said. "You look like you're ready to kill Alex!"

"I'll get to the good part," Amber said, fast-forwarding it again. This time, an angry Maya glared directly into the camera. "How would you like me to come over there and shove that camera down your ratty throat?"

Alex and Morgan began to howl with glee. The videotape

played on as Alex began to shake the camera and said, "Now the camerawoman is quivering with fear because the Great Humanitarian wants to shove the camera down her throat. Please don't hurt me, Great Humanitarian!"

Amber turned off the tape, and she and Maya waited quietly as Alex's and Morgan's laughter ebbed away.

"Sorry, Maya," Morgan said, pulling herself together. "We can edit it and make it look good. Right, Amber?"

"Of course we can," Amber said. "We'll use some of today's tape. I'll take out all the audio portion and rearrange the video clips so it'll be fine. Maybe what you need to do is write your speech, and then we can dub it over the videotape later. How does that sound?"

Maya nodded. *Don't start crying; don't start crying.* "I'm going home now," she said quietly.

chapter.12

Maya spent Sunday afternoon hiding from the world in her sweats and watching TV. CNN had a running story of the Karen Dean-Malloy election campaign. The latest update showed the senator outraged at the negative campaign advertisements from her opponent Rodney Gorman. But the story also quoted Gorman, staunchly denying that the advertisements were written and placed by his campaign. "We've hired private investigators," Gorman said. "We'll release their findings as soon as they're reported to us."

"Oh sure," Maya said to the TV screen. "Like you didn't write those and pay for those attacks yourself?"

Maya couldn't bring herself to work on her own campaign speech. With the videotape turning out to be such a disaster, there was nothing Maya could think of to write about. The dress code was such a difficult issue, and Mrs. Clark still hadn't given them enough details for Maya to form an opinion, let alone defend her opinion to anyone else.

Maya, Morgan, and Jacob were all parked on the sofa channel surfing with the remote. As usual, Jacob was hogging the remote and watching sports highlights. When the phone rang, Morgan waited until the third ring to pick it up.

"Hey," the frazzled voice said. "I'm at the Gnosh. And I'm wading through about 30 gallons of frozen mocha drink—it's all over the floor."

Somehow Dad's machine for making frozen mocha drinks had leaked all night. The floor was completely coated with mocha concentrate.

"I need all three of you down here," Dad said. "With all of us working, it won't take that long to clean up."

Dad rarely ordered the Cross kids to work on Sunday afternoons. With a chorus of moaning and whimpering, all three of them pulled on jackets and shoes and piled into Mr. Beep. The trio drove in a gloomy silence to the restaurant.

When they walked in the back door, Dad had already prepared two steaming buckets of suds and two mops. He handed the mops to Jacob and Maya. "I've only got two mops," Dad announced. "So Morgan can clean out the toasters and roll the silverware into the napkins."

"Hey Dad," Jacob said, plunging his mop into the soapy

water and working the corners of his mouth to keep a straight face. "When did slavery come back in style?"

"Slavery?" Dad pretended to look shocked. "Someday this entire business will belong to you and your sisters. You three are the heirs to the vast Gnosh Pit fortune!"

While Dad and Jacob kept up a steady stream of one-liners, Maya's thoughts wandered to the children of Karen Dean-Malloy. Jason and Hedy were probably spending their weekend in some lush tropical condo or snowboarding at some posh Vermont ski resort. And here Maya was, pushing a mop through an enormous inland sea of mocha concentrate. She could only shake her head and keep mopping.

Without any enthusiasm, Maya logged in to the chat room for the girls' Sunday night cyber visit.

> **nycbutterfly:** every time i try 2 write my campaign speech, it sounds so stupid I have 2 quit!!!!
>
> **faithful1:** U R not going to believe this!!!!! when I checked the school Web site 2nite, some1 had hacked into the site and trashed U!
>
> **nycbutterfly:** what do U mean?
>
> **faithful1:** the hacker wrote: Maya Cross endorses school uniforms!!!!
>
> **nycbutterfly:** what?????????????????

chicChick: U do?

nycbutterfly: NW!!!! how could someone hack into the school Web site?

faithful1: I don't know, has never happened B4! 2morrow I'll check the site at school and try 2 figure it out

TX2step: it's probably that same girl who called the parking police on Maya!

chicChick: who??????

TX2step: brittany mertz!

faithful1: we don't know who did this so let's wait until I can check the Web site 2morrow and figure this out!

On Monday morning, Maya arrived at school to find anti-Maya posters all over the school. The posters' headlines read: "Think About It."

"Maya Cross wants us all to wear uniforms to school. Is this the person you want in student council? Keep your freedoms! Vote for Camille Bates."

"This is the same lie that was printed on the school's Web site," Morgan said, reading the poster alongside Maya.

Amber joined the girls in the hall. "Mrs. Clark said she wants to see us in her office. Camille Bates is already in there."

Amber and Maya walked into Mrs. Clark's office. Camille and Bethany were already seated and staring at the floor.

"Come in," Mrs. Clark said in her official tone. "We have something to discuss."

Amber and Maya sat down and waited. The only sound was the heating system, blowing air from the vents.

"This campaign has gone far enough when it comes to dirty tricks," Mrs. Clark said. "I read those new posters. How do you explain them, Miss Bates?"

Camille looked beaten down, like a prisoner whose head and hands were locked in a pillory. "Mrs. Clark, I swear I don't know where those campaign posters came from. And neither does Bethany. We had nothing to do with this."

Maya was starting to enjoy this. After a weekend of getting yelled at by Coach, ticketed by the parking police, and now being trashed by Camille Bates, Maya was ready for some sympathy.

"I expect both of you to behave in ways that are above this kind of mudslinging," Mrs. Clark said. "If I see any more of this, that candidate will be disqualified. Immediately. Do I make myself clear on this?"

"Yes, Mrs. Clark," Camille said, looking more miserable than Maya had ever seen her.

"Yes, Mrs. Clark," Maya answered, trying to look as somber as possible.

In government class, Mr. Wallace started class by discussing the campaign. But instead of being the big know-it-all, Camille kept a low profile. When asked about the school's Web site, Camille denied having anything to do with the anti-Maya slogans. A few students gave Maya cynical looks. Maya just smiled back and shrugged.

"This is great!" Maya told Amber, digging into her chef salad at lunch. "Everybody feels sorry for me. The tide has turned!"

"I don't know," Amber said, chewing thoughtfully. "I think we ought to stick to the issues and not try to cash in on this latest campaign trick. Maybe it is true. Maybe Camille really didn't know anything about those posters."

Maya was mildly annoyed. "What difference does it make? Her campaign manager endorsed Camille in the school newspaper, and Camille claimed that she didn't know anything about that! And another friend of Camille's called the parking police on Mr. Beep. I'll bet she doesn't know anything about that, either!"

"I'm not saying Camille is perfect," Amber said. "But if we're going to win this election, we need to win it the right way. Have you written your speech for the assembly tomorrow?"

Maya groaned. "I don't have any idea what I want to say in that speech."

"Good," Amber said, handing Maya a stack of papers. "As your campaign manager, I've written a speech that you can use. It just talks about how you would like to serve the school. No cheap shots at Camille Bates."

"Oh, that's just great," Maya said, growing more annoyed. "Camille Bates can take all the cheap shots she wants at me. And

I have to put up with it. And not say a word about it in my campaign speech. Does that sound fair to you?"

"As a matter of fact, it does," Amber said calmly. "If the students vote for you, it'll be because they see that you're a leader worth following. Not because we figured out a better way to trash Camille."

"Whatever," Maya said testily. "Let's just hope that after all of Camille's underhanded tricks, the students can still remember which one of us is the good guy!"

Maya stood up, grabbed her plastic salad bowl, and dumped it in the dish room window. Then she walked into the student center, which by now was papered with campaign signs.

"Hey, good luck, Maya," one girl said to her. "I'm voting for you."

"Thanks," Maya said. "I appreciate that."

Lori Kate came bustling up to Maya, waving a sheaf of papers. "Here are some suggestions for your speech tomorrow. Maybe you can use a few of these points, you know, about the campaign."

"Yeah, thanks," Maya said, pretending to look at the writing before folding the papers in half. "I'll read through these a little later."

"I just know that you're going to win this election," Lori Kate said. "Camille has really pulled some dirty tricks on you."

"Well, that stopped today," Maya said. "Mrs. Clark called us into her office this morning and made it very clear. Any more dirty tricks and the candidate gets disqualified."

"Wow!" Lori Kate exclaimed. "Camille would have to be crazy to try anything else."

"She won't," Maya said. "She's not my favorite person, but Camille is smart enough to know when Mrs. Clark means business. I'm just glad it'll all be over tomorrow."

"Me, too," Lori Kate said. "I can't wait for tomorrow."

As soon as Maya got home from school, she stopped in the kitchen for a handful of carrot sticks. She took the stairs two at a time up to her room, dropping her books on the bed and switching on the computer.

Maya typed in votedean_malloy.org and waited for the site to appear. She double-clicked on the box that read "E-Mail your senator!"

An empty box appeared on the screen. Above it was an American flag that waved choppily back and forth and this message: "Tell Karen Dean-Malloy what is on your mind."

Maya put her fingers on the keyboard to type and then stopped. What should she ask? How could she possibly explain how scared and nervous she felt on the day before the election? Is this the way the senator felt the day before an election?

Dear Ms. Dean-Malloy,

Tomorrow is our school's student council election. This campaign has been very hard, much harder than I thought it would be. Do you ever wonder if being a senator is really worth it? I mean, worth all of the speeches you have to make and the signs and TV advertisements you have to create? Do you ever get sick of the attacks from your opponent? Do you ever get sick of the whole thing?

Sincerely,
Maya Cross

Maya hit *Send* and sat back. A bright shaft of late afternoon sun streamed in from her window and caught Maya's attention. She stood up, stretched, and sauntered to the window. A few fall leaves skittered lightly across the street. This felt like a day from long ago, when Maya spent the hours between school and supper in her favorite place. At that moment, she knew exactly where she needed to go.

Grabbing a jacket from the back porch, Maya pulled her arms through the long sleeves as she made her way past the patio furniture and into the grass. At the back of the lot, away from everything else, sat the playhouse. Maya's grandpa had built it for the three kids one summer when they were still living in New York. Grandpa had surprised them with it when they had come for their annual summer visit.

Maya crouched down and squeezed through the small door. Morgan still used the playhouse to entertain some of the kids she baby-sat, so the little house was still clean inside and even had two baby dolls lying on a blanket in one corner. Maya scooted back into her favorite spot where she could lean against the wall and gaze out the open door.

She chuckled to herself, remembering the day when Grandpa had brought them to the backyard to show them the new playhouse he had built. It was a thing of beauty—white clapboard walls with a real door and two windows with real shutters that closed. And it was just their size.

Even though they were only three, five, and six years old at the time, they wanted to move into the playhouse and sleep in it. The next day, a scary-looking dog had wandered into the backyard. Instead of running to the big house, Jacob, Maya, and Morgan had beat feet to the playhouse and slammed the door behind them as if they were holding off an entire pack of wolves. After that, they had spent the rest of the day pretending that they really were the three little pigs and convincing their grandpa to play the big bad wolf. Their laughter and squeals still rang in Maya's ears.

It feels so safe in here, Maya told herself. *Life was so easy when this playhouse was the center of my world. Why does everything have to change? I don't want Morgan or Jacob to grow up or my parents to grow old. Why do we all have to grow up?*

If I just stay in here, she thought, *maybe the world will stop changing for a few hours.* And so Maya sat perfectly still, listening to the remaining song birds and the few leaves that still rustled in their branches, holding on to the last vestiges of childhood that still lingered in the little house.

When she heard her mother's tires on the gravel driveway and saw the lengthening shadows turning into darkness, Maya knew it was time to go inside and help her mother get dinner ready. Go back and rejoin the real world of high school and homework and Web sites and student council elections.

Before starting dinner, Maya made a quick trip upstairs to her computer to check for any e-mail she might have gotten from the senator. If there was ever a time when Maya needed some answers, or even just a word of encouragement, it was now.

There were no new messages.

That night, Maya lay in bed, trying to fall asleep. Her mind kept returning to Amber's campaign speech, with its quotes on leadership: "A good leader takes a little more than her share of the blame, and a little less than her share of the credit." Another quote from Amber that Maya liked was, "Leaders are ordinary people with extraordinary determination."

Lori Kate's speech sounded the same, until you read between the lines: "I would like to thank all the students who are voting for me. I know that some of the recent campaign tactics have been unworthy of the democratic process. And I think students want a campaign without the dirty tricks and mudslinging we've seen in this election. Please restore honor to student council, and vote for me."

What was so wrong with pointing out that Camille hadn't played fair in this race? It was the truth. What was so wrong with pointing out the truth?

chapter.13

I don't believe it."

"It's true," Morgan said. "Take a look." Morgan held out the Election Issue of *The Eagle's Nest*. On the front page were both candidates' platforms. Maya's was printed just the way she and Amber had written it. But Camille Bates's platform was another matter.

"I believe that only students with A averages should be allowed to attend the prom, play on a sports team, or run for student council," her platform story read. "Why should we allow students who aren't performing well academically to participate in extracurricular activities?"

The platform went on and on like that. Maya read it as she made her way to her locker. Standing by her locker, waiting for her, was Amber.

"What's going on here?" Maya said, waving the newspaper at Amber.

"I don't know," Amber said. "But this platform did not come from Camille Bates. No way."

Just the way Amber said it confirmed Maya's worst fears. "Let's go check our campaign headquarters."

The girls booted up the computer at their headquarters and checked various files, hoping for a clue. But nothing had been added, changed, or deleted.

"I've got to get to my first block," Amber said. "Maybe we can figure out what's going on before the election assembly."

"OK," Maya called. "See you in the gym."

On her way to class Maya passed the room Camille used for campaign headquarters. Maya opened the door and turned on the light. No one was there. If everybody was on their way to class, she might have enough time to look through Camille's computer files.

Maya closed the door and locked it from the inside. Then she sat down and booted up the computer. Clicking on a series of icons, she found Camille's campaign speech and Camille's platform. She double-clicked on the platform, and it came up on the screen. Just as she and Amber had suspected, Camille's real campaign platform was nothing like the version that had been printed in today's election paper.

"This makes no sense," Maya whispered to herself.

When the tardy buzzer rang, Maya nearly jumped out of her

skin with fright. Maya put her hand over her heart and felt how hard it was beating. As she guided the mouse to the *Quit* command on the menu, she noticed an icon for a diskette labeled campaign.

She double-clicked on the icon. A single document opened up. It was a list of ideas:

1. small negative posters to undermine voters' confidence.
2. list negative campaign info on Web site.
3. rewrite platform to alienate voters.
4. dress alike to intimidate the opposition.

The last idea confirmed what Maya had suspected. She knew what she had to do next.

"Yes?" Mrs. Feingold said.

"I was sent to deliver a message for Lori Kate Cox," Maya said from the doorway. "She's wanted in the office."

Lori Kate looked up brightly from her workbook. Mrs. Feingold nodded, and Lori Kate slid her workbook into her book bag, stood up, and trotted outside. Maya began walking down the hall, and Lori Kate ran to catch up.

"What's going on?" she said, her voice filled with glee. "Is Camille in trouble again?"

Maya turned around and looked at Lori Kate. "You did all of this."

Lori Kate grinned. "Have you seen the way the students are treating Camille? Everybody is angry with her!"

"It was you who called the police on my car yesterday," Maya stated, trying to stay calm.

Lori Kate fought back a modest smile. "I did it from a pay phone. And they just took my word for it that I was Brittany Mertz. I knew you would be fighting mad at Camille after that!"

Maya was choking on her own disbelief. "What's wrong with you? Did you think this was the only way I could win this election? By pulling dirty tricks on the other person? And me?"

Lori Kate looked pensive. "No, I didn't think that. But I wanted to make sure you won this election. And Camille is such a pain, I figured you wouldn't mind if I did a few things behind the scenes to wreck her chances. I knew, sooner or later, you'd figure it out. You're a very smart person."

Maya slumped down on a bench next to the drinking fountain. "Oh yeah, I'm really smart. I'm so smart I let you blow this whole election for me."

Lori Kate seemed as unperturbed as she always was. "Well, I think you're a lot smarter than Karen Dean-Malloy."

Maya was now completely lost in this conversation. "And what makes you say that?"

"I guess you didn't watch CNN this morning," Lori Kate said. "Last night, Rodney Gorman announced that he had evidence showing the attacks on Karen Dean-Malloy were coming from her own campaign. This morning she held a news conference. She admitted that the attacks had come from her campaign. But she claims she didn't know anything about it until last night."

Maya was stunned. Her whole world was going down the drain, role model and all.

Lori Kate walked over to Maya and put a friendly hand on her shoulder. "Let's just keep this whole thing between us. You can win this election, and no one will ever know the difference. Everybody already blames Camille for running a dirty tricks campaign. End of story."

Maya looked at Lori Kate in disbelief. "But you said I was a smart person," Maya said. "If I'm such a smart person, I'm going to do what a smart person does when she finds out her entire campaign is one big lie."

Lori Kate looked scared. "You aren't going to tell Mrs. Clark I did this, are you? Because I don't think its fair to blame the whole thing on me. I mean, sure, I came up with a basic overall strategy. And I probably should have gotten your permission on some of the dirty tricks. But I'm not willing to take all of the blame on this. You can't make me take the rap for this whole campaign. I'll deny everything."

Maya sighed and shook her head. "Don't worry. You're not the one in the hot seat. I am."

Maya looked at the hall clock. There were only fifteen minutes until the campaign assembly in the gym. Only fifteen minutes to figure out how to unravel the lies upon lie upon lies.

The gym was filling with students as Maya and the other student council candidates took their seats on the stage. Camille sat on the other side of the stage, a determined look on her face. Neither Camille nor Maya looked at each other. Maya's eyes were glued to the speech notes Amber had prepared.

When all of the students were seated, Mrs. Clark walked to the microphone. "Good morning. Today is Edgewood High School's student council elections. We begin today's events with an assembly. After all the candidates have spoken, students will cast their votes. I'll announce the names of the winners on the public address system later in the day."

Mrs. Clark took her seat on the stage and nodded at Maya.

Maya stood up, smoothed her skirt, and walked to the microphone. She put her notes on the lectern, looked down at them, and then looked out at the gym filled with students.

"I had a speech prepared for today's assembly. But I'm not going to give that speech," Maya said. "Except I think I'll still use this quote: 'A good leader takes a little more than her share of the blame, a little less than her share of the credit.' I'm not so sure if I am a good leader or not. But today, I need to take my share of the blame."

Maya paused to take a deep breath. She felt a balloon inside her chest, full of sorrow and waiting to burst. But for now, she held it tightly under control.

"During this campaign, several dirty tricks were pulled on Camille Bates. And they came directly from my campaign. It really doesn't matter who did them or why they were done. The point is that they came from my campaign. I am truly sorry they happened, and I take full responsibility. And because of those events, I think it's impossible to hold a fair election.

"The only way to make this right is for me to withdraw from this election. So I'm officially stepping down as a candidate for student council. To those of you who supported my campaign, thanks for putting your trust in me. Maybe next time, I'll be more worthy of that trust. Thank you."

Maya picked up her notes and walked out of the gym. The only sound was her footsteps on the gymnasium floor. She kept walking, down the hall, out the student parking entrance, until she found herself opening Mr. Beep's door, and sliding into the driver's seat. She tore the paper election badge off the tiny dashboard, crumpling it into a tiny ball, and leaned her forehead against the steering wheel.

"It's over, Mr. Beep," Maya said softly. "It's all over."

chapter.14

The Gnosh was bustling with its usual after-school crowd. The back booth was particularly noisy.

Right after Maya had given her withdrawal speech, Morgan had telephoned her dad with the news. Dad had called the bakery and ordered a sheet cake that read: "Maya Cross 4 EVER!" Dad had even bought streamers and confetti.

When Maya and Amber arrived for a quiet post-election Coke, they were met with a group of eager, familiar faces: Alex, Morgan, Bren, and Jamie. As soon as Maya sat down, Dad brought out the cake, and the girls showered her with a blizzard of colorful paper.

"Hey!" Maya squealed with surprise. "You guys must have missed the main point of my speech. I dropped out of the race, remember?"

"It doesn't matter," Amber said. "You did the right thing. That's so much better than winning."

"Yeah," Jamie said, grinning shyly. "Maya Cross: The Honest Choice!"

The girls laughed, and Maya gave Jamie a hug. "Thanks."

Dad passed out slices of cake and then returned with a large tray of tumblers and pitchers of soda. "I want to propose a toast."

Everybody took a glass of soda and held it aloft. "To Maya," Dad said, smiling at her, "and whatever career you choose. You'll be the best!"

"Here, here!" Amber said, hoisting her soda.

"Here, here!" the girls echoed.

Maya put her glass down. "Thanks, but I think my next career just might be landscaping. I told Coach I would help him clean up the Habitat yard this weekend. And I promised not to bring a video camera!"

"Here, here!" Alex said, hoisting her glass again. Everybody laughed.

"There's just one thing I don't understand," Maya said. "Why do I feel so good right now? Shouldn't I be miserable? I just told the whole school that I ran a dirty tricks campaign!"

"The reason you feel so good is simple," Amber said. "Camille became a member of student council, but you became a leader worth following. In a way, you both won. Even though your victory will last a lot longer. "

"All I wanted to do was follow in Karen Dean-Malloy's foot-steps," Maya said. "I think I need to find a new role model. Someone who doesn't sabotage her own campaign."

"Speaking of sabotage, has anyone seen Copy Kate Cox?" Alex asked.

"Lori Kate is one strange ranger," Alex said. "I just don't understand it. Why did she do all of those wacky things?"

Maya shrugged. "She's not so bad. Lori Kate's a hard worker, no question about it. Next time she'll make a great campaign manager. Or maybe even a candidate."

"I think I'm going to miss having her around," Bren said, playfully elbowing Maya. "You've got to admit it. She's a great dresser!"

"I'm glad you feel that way, Bren," Alex said and winked. "I just saw her walk in here, and she's wearing your outfit!"

Bren was halfway out of her seat, craning her neck both ways, before she realized that Alex had gotten her once again.

Net Ready, Set, Go!

I hope my words and thoughts please you.
Psalm 19:14

The characters of TodaysGirls.com chat online in the safest—and maybe most fun—of all chat rooms! They've created their own private Web site and room! Many Christian teen sites allow you to create your own private chat rooms, and there are other safe options.

Work with your parents to develop a list of safe, appropriate chat rooms. Earn Internet freedom by showing them you can make the right choices. *Honor your father and your mother (Deuteronomy 5:16).*

Before entering a chat room, you'll select a user name. Although you can use your real name, a nickname is safer. Most people choose one that says something about who they are, like Amber's name, faithful1. Don't be discouraged if the name you select is already taken. You can use a similar one by adding a number at its end.

No one will notice your grammar in a chat room. Don't worry if you spell something wrong or forget to capitalize. Some people even misspell words on purpose. You might see a sentence like How R U?

But sometimes it's important to be accurate. Web site and e-mail addresses must be exact. Pay close attention to whether letters are upper- or lowercase. Remember that Web site addresses don't use some punctuation marks, such as hyphens and apostrophes. (That's why the "Today's" in TodaysGirls.com has no apostrophe!) And instead of spaces between words, underlines are often used to_make_a_space. And sometimes words just run together like onebigword.

When you're in a chat room, remember real people are typing the words that appear on your screen. Treat them with the same respect you expect from them. Don't say anything you wouldn't want repeated in Sunday school. *Do for other people what you want them to do for you (Luke 6:31).*

Sometimes people say mean, hurtful things—things that make us angry. This can happen in chat rooms, too. In some chat rooms, you can highlight a rude person's name and click a button that says, "ignore," which will make his or her comments disappear from your screen. You always have the option to switch rooms or sign off. If a particular person becomes a continual problem, or if someone says something especially vicious, you should report this problem user to the chat service. *Ask God to bless those who say bad things to you. Pray for those who are cruel (Luke 6:28–29).*

Remember that Internet information is not always factual. Whether you're chatting or surfing Web sites, be skeptical about information and people. Not everything on the Internet is true. You don't have to be afraid of the Internet, but you should always be cautious. Practice caution with others even in Christian chat rooms.

It's OK to chat about your likes and dislikes, but *never* give out personal information. Do not tell anyone your name, phone number, address, or even the name of your school, team, church, or neighborhood. Be cautious. . . . *You will be like sheep among wolves. So be as smart as snakes. But also be like doves and do nothing wrong. Be careful of people (Matthew 10:16–17).*

N 2 DEEP & STRANGER ONLINE
16/junior
e-name: faithful1
best friend: Maya
site area: Thought for the Day

Confident. Caring. Swimmer. Single-handedly built
TodaysGirls.com Web site. Loves her folks.
Big brother Ryan drives her nuts! Great friend.
Got a problem? Go to Amber.

AMBER
THOMAS

JAMIE CHANDLER

PLEASE REPLY! & PORTRAIT OF LIES
15/sophomore
e-name: rembrandt
best friend: Bren
site area: Artist's Corner

Quiet. Talented artist. Works at the Gnosh Pit
after school. Dad left when she was little.
Helps her mom with younger sisters Jordan and
Jessica. Baby-sits for Coach Short's kids.

ALEX DIAZ

4GIVE & 4GET & TANGLED WEB
14/freshman
e-name: TX2step
best friend: Morgan
site area: Entertain Us

Spicy. Hot-tempered Texan. Lives with grandparents because
of parents' problems. Won state in freestyle swimming at her
old school. Snoops. Into everything. Breaks the rules.

POWER DRIVE & R U 4 REAL?
16/junior
e-name: nycbutterfly
best friend: Amber
site area: What's Hot—What's Not

Fashion freak. Health nut. Grew up in New York City.
Small town drives her crazy. Loves to dance.
Dad owns the Gnosh Pit. Little sis Morgan is also
a TodaysGirl.

MAYA CROSS

BREN MICKLER

UNPREDICTABLE & LUV@FIRST SITE
15/sophomore
e-name: chicChick
best friend: Jamie
site area: Smashin' Fashion

Funny. Popular. Outgoing. Spaz. Cheerleader. Always late.
Only child. Wealthy family. Bren is chatting—
about anything, online and off, except when
she's eating junk food.

MORGAN
CROSS

FUN E-FARM & CHAT FREAK
14/freshman
e-name: jellybean
best friend: Alex
site area: Feeling All Write

The Web-ster. Spends too much time online. Overalls.
M&M's. Swim team. Tries to save the world. Close to her
family—when her big sister isn't bossing her around.

Cyber Glossary

Bounced mail An e-mail that has been returned to its sender.

Chat A live conversation—typed or spoken through microphones—among individuals in a chat room.

Chat room A "place" on the Internet where individuals meet to "talk" with one another.

Crack To break a security code.

Download To receive information from a more powerful computer.

E-mail Electronic mail sent through the Internet.

E-mail address An Internet address where e-mail is received.

File Any document or image stored on a computer.

Floppy disk A small, thin plastic object that stores information to be accessed by a computer.

Hacker Someone who tries to gain unauthorized access to another computer or network of computers.

Header Text at the beginning of an e-mail that identifies the sender, subject matter, and the time at which it was sent.

Home page A Web site's first page.

Internet A worldwide electronic network that connects computers to each other.

Link Highlighted text or a graphic element that may be clicked with the mouse in order to "surf" to another Web site or page.

Log on/Log in To connect to a computer network.

Modem A device that enables computers to exchange information.

The Net The Internet.

Newbie A person who is learning or participating in something new.

Online To have Internet access. Can also mean to use the Internet.

Surf To move from page to page through links on the Web.

Upload To send information to a more powerful computer.

The Web The World Wide Web or WWW.